SIX BREWS UNDER

ORCHARD HOLLOW

A.N. SAGE

OLIVERHEBERBOOKS

Cover Art by Cauldron Press

Published by Oliver-Heber Books

0 9 8 7 6 5 4 3 2 1

CONTENTS

CHAPTER
1

The morning sun cast a warm glow through the windows of Bean Me Up, spreading long shadows across the cozy coffee shop. In the heart of Orchard Hollow, a small town nestled among tall cliffs and a sun-filled seaside, the aroma of freshly ground coffee beans wafted through the air, enticing locals and travelers alike.

I dashed around the bustling shop, my apron fluttering behind me like a caffeinated cape. With a whirlwind of efficiency, I brewed, frothed, and served an array of concoctions, each one crafted with care and precision. But amidst the flurry of orders and the rhythmic hum of the espresso machine, there was a mischievous presence stirring beneath the surface.

Perched upon a stool behind the counter, Harry Houdini surveyed the chaos with a mischievous glint in his masked eyes. Over the last month, he has become somewhat of an unconventional pet for a coffee shop, but I had a soft spot for the quirky raccoon, so he was here to stay. Except when he caught a ride back to my house with whoever was unlucky enough to go in that direction and leave their car doors open.

As I juggled a tray laden with steaming cups of coffee, Harry seized the opportunity to pounce. With lightning speed, he darted across the counter, his tiny paws swiping at a stray pastry left unattended.

"Piper, look out!" Rory, my assistant, exclaimed, pointing at the thieving raccoon.

I spun around just in time to catch Harry in the act, his guilty expression giving him away. "Harry!" I scolded, swiping at the bugger with a wet towel. "You know better than to steal pastries before rush hour."

Harry blinked innocently, crumbs clinging to his whiskers as he attempted to feign innocence. A few more Bambi-like eye blinks and he was off, rushing somewhere else to cause his brand of chaos, I bet.

The bell rang as the cafe door swung open and a group of tourists stepped inside. Their eyes widened in surprise, taking in every spacey-themed detail of Bean Me Up. I stretched over the front counter, smiling. This part of the job would never get old. Neither would being able to support myself off a cafe I opened on a whim, but here we were.

"You want me to get them?" Rory, my only employee, asked.

Her purple hair was tied in a high top knot, which she bedazzled with several sparkly clips. Today, Rory wore ripped denim overalls under her cafe apron, which struck me as the most uncomfortable attire. I would never understand teenage fashion for as long as I lived. Despite being forty-one and vividly remembering my own teen years, I was always a kid that favored comfort above all else. Judging by Rory's three-inch platform boots that she wore for a six-hour shift—we didn't have that in common.

The young witch tossed a chocolate-covered espresso bean into her mouth and smiled. "I got these guys," she repeated. "I want to get faster with my latte skills. The new one you added last week is a lot!"

"The Coco-latte?" I asked. Giggling in my head. I specifically added that drink as a nod to the first vacation I was taking in years. Coconut milk, vanilla, maple syrup... What's not to love? I tamped down my glee. "I think it's worth the extra effort. How about you, Cilia?"

Turning my attention to my friend and another local witch, I quirked a brow and grinned mischievously. As expected, Cilia got my hint and went along seamlessly. She tucked a hair that escaped her messy bob behind an ear and trained her hazel eyes on Rory. "Agreed. Actually, I might get a cup of it myself since you're going to be making a batch."

"You two are the worst!" Rory exclaimed, smacking her aunt with a tea towel before sauntering away to greet our customers.

While she handled the drinks, I allowed myself a moment of peace before the cafe picked up for the afternoon. Across the counter from me, Cilia toyed with a spaceship napkin holder and bit her bottom lip. Rory's aunt was a witch not to be trifled with, but moments like this I remembered just how great she was. Despite her boss, our local vampire boss lady, finding herself on the other side of being alive, leaving Cilia to deal with running the hotel, she still made time to hang out with me.

I looked around the cafe to make sure Isabella Beaumont's ghost wasn't skulking around. Finding the coast clear, I faced Cilia. "How are things going with the hotel?"

"Oh, you mean the hot mess Isabella dumped on my lap before she kicked the bucket? Just dandy."

I grimaced. "That rough, huh?"

"You can say that twice! I know I shouldn't complain since she pretty much gifted me an entire business, but I'm in over my head," Cilia said solemnly. "I don't know the first thing about running that place." She paused. "I must sound awful. It's not Isabella's fault I'm lost."

Glancing around again, I rolled my shoulders and sat up taller. "That, and it's not like she had other options," I reminded Cilia. "Considering she didn't exactly choose to leave the plane of the living."

"Right. Right, of course," Cilia agreed. Her gaze followed mine, flicking around the cafe. "Is she...?"

I shook my head. "All clear. I haven't seen Isabella since she left with my mother to follow the Sisters of the River. As a matter of fact, I should probably check in later, see if they uncovered anything useful."

After what happened to her boss, it only made the most sense for me to come clean with Cilia. I had to admit, the more time passed, the more I got used to having half of Hades' bloodline and magic coursing through me. And I was even getting better at controlling my powers. It had been days since a rift to the Underworld opened and Stella, my ghost familiar, and I worked on daily meditation to clear my mind so I didn't accidentally summon my father. I did still keep an eye out for any lingering ghosts since it seemed my powers were growing—a thought I tried not to dwell on. If I was stronger, that meant Hades was, too. Who knew what dear old Dad had planned for the future.

Especially if Mom and Isabella couldn't stop the Sisters, his wicked follower coven, from raising the ancient deity with their ritual.

"Did Sylvie mention if the Sisters figured out what happened here?" Cilia asked.

It was a valid question and one I should have asked Mom myself. I felt foolish for not thinking of it the last time she called. After all, the entire point of her going back to the coven was to sleuth out how much they knew of what went down in Orchard Hollow when one of their head witches came for Mom and her partner. Poor Mrs. Cevil paid the price for plotting against the witches. My heart still ached for the old woman each time I passed by the bakery on my way to work.

Stomach rumbling at the thought of baked goods, I took a sip of my coffee and faced Cilia. "She didn't say anything," I told her. "But I'm assuming no news is good news. I have enough to worry about as it is."

"You mean your romantic getaway?" the witch asked, her eyebrows wiggling.

I smacked her arm playfully. "Stop it! I'm already a nervous wreck about the trip with Joe without you making it worse."

Cilia reached into her purse and yanked out a ball of green fabric. She tossed it over the counter. I scrambled to catch it before it fell into my coffee cup.

Unfolding the ball, my jaw unhinged in a gasp. In my hands was a long, sexy cover up with an intricate pattern of ivy leaves sewn into the most buttery silk I'd ever touched.

"A little gift for the road," Cilia explained. "I spelled it with anti-anxiety runes in the stitching. I figured you could use some calming down."

"Cilia! This is stunning. You shouldn't have!"

The witch batted me away, settling back in her chair. "Nonsense. When I saw it, I knew you had to wear it. That green is the perfect shade for your hair and complexion. Besides, considering how much you're doing to save the world from the literal God of Death, I think you could use a moment to enjoy yourself. Have you packed yet?"

"Not even a little," I admitted. "I hadn't gone on a trip in ages and Joe still won't tell me where we're going."

"All you know is that it's an island, right?"

I nodded. Joe, my vampire boyfriend, was keeping the details of our trip hush-hush. A part of me was grateful for the surprise and loved how much work he put into planning this for us. Another part of me absolutely hated not being able to prepare better. I had packed and unpacked Gran's vintage suitcase four times, unable to decide. It didn't help that my ghost familiar had an opinion on every piece I tried to take with me. Stella Rutherford didn't agree with any of the outfits I had in my closet.

I got tired of reminding her that not all of us had an unlimited budget to spend on clothes. The comments only earned me crude remarks about how much time I'd be spending out of my clothes on the trip.

Bristling, I eyed the cafe. *Where is that ghost, anyway?* I hadn't seen Stella all morning and usually that meant one of two things: either she was mad at me for no good reason or she was off doing whatever it was rich ladies did with their afterlife. Based on historical facts, neither option fared well for me in the end.

I popped the last bite of my bagel in my mouth and downed the remaining coffee. "Honestly, I'm happy to go wherever at this point. It would be lovely to pretend to be normal for a week." In my excitement at thinking about the trip, I knocked my elbow into the empty plate on the counter and sent it crashing to the ground. Groaning, I cleaned up the mess and avoided Rory's frustrated glares from behind the espresso. "That is, if I can manage from messing up as I usually do."

"Stop it!" Cilia exclaimed. "You're too hard on yourself. I'm sure once you're lounging on a beach with your yummy boyfriend, all those nerves will melt away."

"Either that or I ruin our entire vacation by falling into a manhole," I countered.

Across from me, Cilia pretended to fall over, and we broke into laughter loud enough to earn us a dramatic eye roll from Rory. As we laughed, a commotion sounded from the back office, putting a pause to our joy. The hairs on the back of my neck stood up straight. I met Rory's questioning glance with a shrug and a wave of the hand, letting her know I got it.

"What was that?" Cilia asked.

"The Bean Me Up Menace," I replied, already on my feet.

Leaving a confused Cilia at the table, I skirted around the small crowd of customers waiting for their drinks and headed for the office. The door's frosted glass made it impossible to see inside, but I had the feeling that if I was right in guessing the intruder, I already knew what I was about to walk in on. Glancing over my shoulder, I checked to make certain no one was watching and called forth my magic. My fingers buzzed with energy as the electricity hiding in my blood crept to the surface. Lips twitching into a smile, I pressed a glowing blue hand to the door and swung it open.

As suspected, the office was overturned.

"For the love of coffee!" I shouted, my blue fist waving in the air. "Harry Houdini!"

Paper coffee cups spread all around me on the floor and I had to skip over them in order to avoid crushing the last remnants of our supplies. There was a shredded stack of napkins under my desk and a trail of crumbs leading from the stocking shelf to the back door. My eyes drifted up to the shelf and I scowled. The monster got into the cookies again. I was sure the barrier I had created around all the edible stock was enough to keep the raccoon away, but it seemed there was no getting in the way of Harry's snacks.

I hated to think it, but it may have been better when he lived at the farmhouse. At least when he broke into the cupboards, I didn't have to think about my business going under.

Frown deepening, I followed the cookie trail to the back alley, where I knew the rascal would be hiding away with his loot. Maybe I'd get lucky and manage to steal back a box he hadn't torn apart yet. As I walked out, a sudden flash of finding Daniel's lifeless body ripped through me and I shuddered, looking around cautiously.

My shoulders slumped in relief. The alley was empty. There was no sign of the raccoon or my cookies, but at least I wouldn't stumble on a dead body today. It was frightening to think how often that happened recently.

After one more quick scan of the alley, I gave up

the search and turned on my heels to march back inside. My attention landed on Gran's gold vintage watch on my wrist. I hurried my pace. It was almost lunch time which meant the rush of locals and tourists was on its way. If I moved fast enough, I might be able to close up early for the evening.

The conversation with Cilia put a pep in my step and as I made my way to the front of the cafe, butterflies swarmed my belly. One more night to pack before we fly out.

The corners of my eyes crinkled; it was refreshing to stress over something as simple as packing for a change.

Rolling my shoulders, I shook off the remnants of my lingering magic and opened the office door. I couldn't wait to be done with the day so I could rush home. *Umbrella drinks and tropical beaches here I come!*

CHAPTER 2

The zipper struggled with the swell of the suitcase, busting at the seams. I plonked on top of the old bag and ground my teeth into a fine pulp as I wrestled it closed. Sweat beaded on my brow and fell into my eyes. I scowled, blinking away the stinging, and continued to work. Fifteen minutes later, my fingers were red and swollen, but the stupid bag was shut.

I stood up slowly and backed away to inspect it. "This won't do."

The suitcase looked like it would explode if someone breathed near it. I could already see the metal handle of the zipper start to come undone and winced, picturing all my belongings flying out like some sort of poorly scripted comedy movie.

"You'll be better off using a garbage bag."

I spun on my heels to face my ghost familiar, glaring at me from the foot of the bed. Her KHOL-lined eyes rolled down my body, and she cringed at the sight of the sweatsuit I wore tonight. Stella's shoulders sagged, her sheer gray body floating toward the bursting suitcase on the floor. "Please tell me you're leaving whatever that outfit is, at home," she said.

"I was thinking of wearing it on the plane," I teased. "Comfy chic and all."

"So help me, Piper, if you use the word chic to describe your monstrous fashion one more time..."

Stella turned up her nose in concentration, then, when she'd built up enough strength, kicked the side of the suitcase. The zipper groaned from the impact and I took a step back when I saw it tear apart. Clothes spilled out of the bag, covering my bedroom floor in a mess of colors and textures. Shuddering, Stella peeled her gaze away from the mess to face me head on. "Please never pack without me again."

I used my foot to drag the clothes into a pile and sat on the edge of the bed. Outside, a tree branch poked its fingers against the window, rapping away a melody to the gusts of wind making it sway. The sun had long set and I could feel the chill in the air in my very bones. Orchard Hollow was in full winter mode, and it was making me all the more excited to get away. Warm weather and days full of sunshine were exactly what I needed to get my mind off everything going on.

On my lap, my fingers tingled. I looked down at the magic gathering there. Shaking it off, I met Stella's worried gaze.

"It's nothing," I told the ghost.

"Looks like something to me," she argued. "Are you sure you'll be fine for a week on your own?"

Biting my lip, I stretched my legs out in front of me and sighed. "I'm not a child," I said. "And Joe will be there if there are any magic mishaps."

I wiggled my fingers for extra emphasis.

"Save those moves for the bedroom."

"Gross, Stella!" I yelled. When the ghost wasn't looking, I swiped a pillow off the bed and tossed it at her. The faux-fur square ripped through her body, landing on top of clothes pile on the other side. Stella yelped. I laughed under my breath. "You deserved that."

She grinned. "Possibly. Any word from Sylvie and the other yet?"

The other was Isabella Beaumont, or her ghost in this case. It had been weeks since she came to me after her death, and Stella was still refusing to accept her existence. It was as though they had some afterlife standoff that I was caught in the middle of. When Isabella had suggested she leave with my mother, I was relieved. As much as I wanted to figure out my Hades magic, having her around put Stella on edge and I had to think of my familiar first. Even if she refused to tell me what her problem was.

Shrugging, I side-eyed Stella. "Nothing much. Last time Mom called, she only had a few minutes to talk, and I hadn't seen Isabella return yet," I said. "She's probably busy keeping an eye out for my reckless mother."

"Right. And the Sisters had no clue what you two did to one of their own?"

"Send her into the Underworld, you mean?" Goosebumps formed on my arms when I remembered shoving the head witch that came after Mom and me into the rift. Even though time had passed, I still had nightmares about it. Sure, she was a heartless killer, but I was never big on an eye for an eye. Using my magic to hurt another crossed all types of lines, whether it was self-defense or not. For the first time since I discovered the history of my Hades ancestry, I wondered how much my father and I truly had in common.

A gray hand waved before my eyes. "Hello? You still here?"

"Yep," I told Stella. "And no, the Sisters assumed

Cassandra Prude went into hiding. Mom did a great job spinning the story to give the coven enough information that they knew she killed on their behalf, but not anything that could tie her back to us. I think having the paper trail of their operation in the last twenty years that Isabella discovered helped. Gave Mom more to work with to spin the lies."

At the mention of Isabella's name, my familiar's eyes rolled backward.

"What is your issue with the vampire, anyway?" I asked.

Stella turned her body away from me, harrumphing. "Never liked the woman, that's all."

"You sure? Because it seems that you might be a little jealous."

While I wasn't paying attention, a flicker of movement flashed in my periphery and I was bashed on the back of the head with a ball of socks. I ground my teeth and turned toward Stella's cocky grin. "Okay fine!" I exclaimed, my hands up in surrender. "But if you ever decide to be an adult and talk about what's bothering you, I'm here for it."

A burst of bright light flashed outside the window and we jumped. The window rattled, the glass shaking so violently I thought it might break. Panicking, I looked at Stella, whose chin nodded in the direction of my hands. My focus landed on my lap and the glowing fingers resting there.

"Not again," I groaned.

The air rippled and tore apart like a zipper opening. I briefly recalled the zipper on the suitcase and laughed under my breath before jumping to my feet. As I stood, the rift between our world and my father's realm widened and I caught a glimpse of something zooming by on the other side. We still had no idea what it was I kept seeing in the rifts, spirits or monsters, but whatever it was, it couldn't get out.

Nothing from the dark realm could make it to our world or it would end in disaster. At least, that's what Mom kept telling me. For some reason, I wasn't so certain I believed her. After all, my father was inside the rifts and I refused to believe that I could come from someone dead-set on ending our existence.

It was likely all a simple misunderstanding.

Sure, he had the Sisters of the River, the world's most mysterious and dark coven working to free him, but still... My gaze flicked to Stella. Technically, she belonged in the Underworld with dear old Dad and there was nothing evil about Stella Rutherford.

"Are these rifts making you lose brain cells?" the ghost asked urgently. "Why are you frozen? Close it!"

Annoying? Yes. Evil? Not so much.

Shaking off my thoughts, I rushed toward the rift and concentrated on keeping my magic solid. My hands shook as I raised them higher and brought them toward the opening. Inside me, the pull I often felt when I was close to a rift intensified and I bit down on my tongue until I tasted iron. Grimacing, I thrust my palms out and pushed the wild electricity coursing through me outward. Sparks ignited on my fingertips and lightning shot out from my skin and into the darkness ahead.

A hiss filled the air as the shadowy creature I saw before got nicked by my magic. I repeated the motion, pushing more of my power into the rift until I saw the opening begin to stitch together. The rift grew smaller and smaller before my eyes while I struggled to stay on track.

When the final remnant of the Underworld vanished, I slumped my shoulders and backed away. Sweat rolled down my brow and fell into my eyes. I swiped at them with the fleshy parts of my palm, wincing at the stinging left behind.

"They're getting tougher to close," I whispered.

"Or you're getting weaker," Stella suggested. "It's possible this vacation will be the ticket you need to get your mojo back."

I shook my head furiously. "My mojo is not the problem. It's him. Hades. He's getting stronger. I can feel it every time a rift opens. Soon, I won't be able to keep him at bay."

"He can't cross over without the ritual the Sisters are planning and not before the blood moon."

Nodding, I sagged against the antique dresser in my room, looking at the carnage on the floor. "Right," I agreed. "We still have time. Which is more than I can say for my packing."

Tsking, Stella swung her arm over the floor and toward the closet. Her eyes narrowed, mischief glistening in their depths. "Must I do everything around here? Fine. Take all the clothes you planned to bring with you and put them in a pile over there," she instructed.

"Then what?"

"Light a match," Stella teased. "But seriously, Piper, if we are going to make the flight tomorrow, we have our work cut out for us."

My brow quirked at her words. "We?"

"Obviously," the ghost said incredulously. "You didn't think I'd let you have all the fun? My transparent self could use with a tan." As she moved toward my closet, I heard her mumble, "Let's hope no one dies on the plane."

Forcing myself not to start an argument, I watched as Stella selected items for me to pack and folded them neatly into the suitcase. Before long, I had all I needed for the trip and Stella agreed that if anything was missing, I could always buy it there. With my clothes packed, I bid Stella goodnight and turned in, vowing to get a good night's rest before the big day tomorrow. Joe was coming by at six with a car and I knew that it would take some time for me to settle.

Especially considering how much Stella's last comment weighed on my mind. Because let's face it, knowing my luck, there truly was a chance I'd stumble on a dead body mid-flight.

CHAPTER 3

"Is this it?" Joe asked as he hoisted my suitcase into the trunk of the cab. "You pack light."

Shrugging, I turned to look at Stella over my shoulder, who nodded her approval. Apparently, there was nothing worse than over-packing for a romantic getaway. As Stella so expertly put it last night, "If you need clothes, you're doing it wrong."

I smiled at Joe and wiped away the snowflakes gathering on the tips of my lashes. The weather turned drastically overnight and a frigid frost enveloped Orchard Hollow like a snowy glove. The first snowfall was always beautiful in our little town; white-capped mountain tops on one side and the hum of the sea on the other. It was so spectacular I almost hated to leave.

Icy wind raked its fingers through my hair, its force making me trip and slide across the gravel until my body crashed into the side of the car with a thud. I chuckled, my cheeks burning red.

On second thought, I couldn't wait for warmer weather.

I climbed into the backseat after Joe and settled in. "This will be fun. Thank you for taking us."

"Wait until you see the villa," Joe said. "You're going to love it." He looked around the car with a grin. "You too, Stella."

Hearing her name, my familiar popped her head around from the passenger side of the cab. I noted her body was almost completely solid and my shoulders sagged in relief. Even Stella was excited about the trip.

She crooked a brow at Joe. "I'll be the judge of that, lover boy."

"She says she can't wait," I told Joe. Then, fixing my familiar with a death glare, added, "I'm sure the villa you rented is breathtaking."

"Oh, I wouldn't go that far," Joe said. "But it is right on the water, so we can take walks every night. And I heard there's a seafood place down the beach that is to die for."

I cringed at his choice of words, my eyes not leaving Stella. "Sounds lovely," I said through clenched teeth.

Call me boring, but I wanted nothing to do with anything worth dying for. I'd had enough death in the recent while to last me a lifetime. And considering what we had to look forward to with the Sisters, I had the anxious feeling that more darkness was headed our way. This trip with Joe was going to be beneficial in more than one way. Perhaps a change of scenery would help me brainstorm ideas on how Mom and I could put an end to the Sisters' plans without anyone getting hurt. Or how I could have a normal conversation with my father. Heck, at this point, I'd settle for a good night's rest where I didn't toss and turn, my eyes wide as moons and staring at the ceiling.

Joe's arm snaked around my shoulders as the cab took a sharp turn.

That is, if I managed to go a week without messing up.

With Stella quiet in the front and the warmth of Joe's body pressed into mine, I relaxed, my eyes slowly closing. My head rested on his wide shoulders and I let the movement of his chest as he breathed lull me into a much needed power nap. By the time the cab came to a stop in the airport parking lot, I was fast asleep, with a little drool dripping from my lips.

"I'll get our bags," Joe said.

While he climbed out of the cab, I took the chance to wipe the sleep from my eyes and mouth.

"Classy," Stella noted, floating to stand beside me. "I'll see you in there."

With that, the ghost was gone.

My gaze traveled past the glass doors and into the belly of the airport. Since Orchard Hollow was off the map, we had to travel into the city to catch our flight. King City was nothing like our quaint little town. The hustle and bustle of city living rang out around me and I was shoulder-checked at least twice while simply standing in place. I watched a mother drag a screaming toddler past me, her face the epitome of humiliation. Behind her, the dad hoisted two large bags and followed them in, his eyes scanning the airport for directions.

"Ready?"

I looked up at Joe. "Let's go."

Joe navigated through the maze that was the King City Airport with ease. He zigged and zagged like someone who worked in these high-ceilinged halls and I had to jog to keep up as he led us through the security gates. Sometimes I forgot that Joe wasn't an Orchard Hollow native like me and had spent most of his life in the city. Being an ex-lawyer, he probably had his fair share of business trips and knew the airport like the back of his vampire hand.

We passed another security point and Joe dropped our bags off, rushing toward me. "Finally," he said, rubbing his muscled arms. His green eyes locked on mine. "Want to get breakfast?"

Nodding, I let him take my hand and lead us to a nearby restaurant that was surprisingly empty, considering how many people were flying this morning. We found an adorable booth in the back and by the time our breakfast arrived, all my nerves had evaporated. Instead, eagerness filled my belly. I sipped on somewhat decent coffee while Joe told me a funny story from his past.

My chest warmed. Oyster Bay. Joe had finally unsealed his lips on the way here and spilled the beans about where we were going. One quick search on my phone and I instantly knew I was going to love it there. The island was spectacular. I couldn't wait to get there.

Unfortunately, my bladder was equally impatient. An announcement filled the air to let us know our flight was getting ready to board. I sucked down the last of the coffee as Joe settled the bill. My head spun around in search of the nearest bathroom, spotting one close to the gate.

"I'll be right back," I told Joe.

He nodded and leaned in to place the softest of kisses on my cheek before dashing off toward the gate, leaving me alone. Not wasting any time, I rushed toward the bathroom, relieved to find it empty. At least

I wasn't going to keep the plane from taking off while I waited in line. I bolted for the closest stall and hurried myself along, listening for another announcement from the gate agents. When the high-pitched voice of an agent echoed through the bathroom, my heart leaped into my throat.

Moving at the speed of light, I burst from the stall and clambered out. My body tensed, legs skidding to a clumsy stop inches away from a massive rift in the air. I paused to take a breath. *Not now!* In front of me, the rift spread wider until I couldn't see the wall-to-wall mirror behind it. I glanced at my hands, now covered in electric magic. In my panic to pee faster, I didn't even notice them.

Why today of all days?

Eyes rolling, I started the process of closing the rift.

"Hello, daughter dearest."

The hairs on the rear of my neck stood on edge as my father's voice boomed through the rift and filled the empty bathroom. I swallowed the growing lump in my throat, eyes flicking to my magic-infused hands. Would closing the rift to the Underworld be the same thing as slamming a door in your dad's face? I didn't have a very rebellious teenage past, but I was pretty certain that if I continued what I was doing a second ago, Hades would not be impressed.

Lowering my arms, I watched as the rift stopped shrinking before me. "Um, hi, there," I said. "Not to be rude, but I am in a bit of a hurry."

"What is time, really? Nothing for the likes of us."

I looked down at my watch, the second hand ticking by quickly. "Maybe so," I replied, steeling my trembling voice. "Except I'm about to miss a flight, so time is quite literally of the essence."

A hearty laugh hit my face as Hades chuckled on the other side of the rift.

"Yes, of course," he said. "I wouldn't want to interrupt your vacation."

"How did you—"

"I know all, daughter dearest," Hades warned.

My throat was suddenly tight and full. I scanned the bathroom for any sign of Stella, but she was nowhere to be found. Which, in this particular case, may have been for the best. My familiar didn't belong in the land of the living and I wasn't sure what the rift, or my father, would do with her if she was nearby. I shuddered, refusing to think of it.

Finding some courage, I folded my arms over my chest and exhaled. "Was there something you needed?"

"Oh, there are many things I require..."

I gulped. "Such as?"

The air between me and the rift rippled. I felt the

pull of the Underworld grip my heart. My body moved against all logic, inching closer to the rift. Closer to my father. I buried the heels of my shoes into the floor and grit my teeth. *Not today, Satan.*

"All in due time," Hades replied. It took him so long to answer, I nearly forgot the question. For a moment, I wondered if there was a communication delay between our two realms, then quickly laughed it off internally. This was magic, dark magic, not a phone line. Sensing my hesitation, Hades said, "Once we are bound, it will be easier to communicate."

Bound? Was he for real? As far as I recalled, I hadn't agreed to be bound to anyone, especially not to my never-present father, who was the freaking God of the Underworld. Besides, from what Mom explained, in order for Hades to cross into our realm, he needed a vessel. If by bound he meant that I would give my body up for him to hitch a ride in, the man was delusional.

I opened my mouth to speak, but Hades beat me to it.

"Enjoy your time away," he purred. "I shall be with you soon."

The rift shut with violent speed and the blast catapulted me backward. My shoulders slammed into the hand dryer, turning it on. As it whirred to life, the air threw my hair around my face until it was a knotted mess. I brushed it back with my hands and washed them before running out the door. As I neared Joe, embarrassment clawed its way up my chest. *I probably look like a disaster now.*

"Missed you," Joe said, reaching for my hand. "Did you change your hair? It looks nice."

"He's lying. You look like you should be committed."

Eyes narrowed to a pin, I spun to my familiar, my fist shaking in her ghostly face. "And where were you, exactly? I had to deal with Hades alone!"

"Hades?" Joe asked, his brow creased.

I patted his arm and continued to march down the narrow jetway leading to the plane. Behind us, the family I saw earlier, wrestled their children into a straight line. My body stiffened, and I took a deep breath, willing my brain to stop working overtime. "I'll fill you in on the plane," I told Joe. "Let's enjoy the flight."

A group of flight attendants gathered in the doorway and butterflies fluttered their wings in my belly. *Here we go...*

CHAPTER 4

The drive from the airport was a sensory overload, a symphony of sights and sounds that enveloped me from the moment we exited the terminal. As we ventured onto the island's roads, each bend revealed a new panorama of beauty. Towering palm trees danced in the gentle breeze, their fronds swaying gracefully against the backdrop of blue skies. The air was thick with the salty tang of the sea, mingling with the sweet scent of tropical blossoms that lined the roadside.

As we approached Oyster Bay, the landscape seemed to shift into a tranquil oasis, a sanctuary from the hustle and bustle of everyday life. Joe's descriptions on the plane ride over painted a picture of serenity, and now, seeing it with my own eyes, I couldn't help but be captivated. The bay stretched out before us, its waters shimmering like liquid sapphire under the golden rays of the sun. Along the winding roads that led through the heart of the island, there was a noticeable absence of tourist activity, lending an air of exclusivity to this hidden gem.

Downtown, where the quaint charm of the island met the sparkling sea, stood a solitary cruise ship, its sleek silhouette a stark contrast against the vast expanse of ocean. The beach, framed by powdery white sands, beckoned with its promise of solitude and relaxation. A handful of sun-seekers dotted the shoreline, their silhouettes casting long shadows in the soft afternoon light. Despite the presence of the cruise ship and the few visitors scattered along the beach, there was an undeniable sense of tranquility that enveloped the scene, as if time itself had slowed to a languid pace in this idyllic corner of the world.

We drove by another small dock hidden away behind a few tall trees and Joe pointed to it eagerly. "That's where we have to go to get to Turtle Cove."

"The what and the who now?"

Joe chuckled. "Turtle Cove. It's a small island off the mainland. Apparently there are hundreds of iguanas living there and if we arrive in time, we get to feed them."

I bristled in my seat, unsure. Though I loved all animals, I had never seen an iguana up close, and the idea of feeding one was giving me some mild anxiety. I faked a smile for Joe's sake and followed his gaze to the tiny piece of land not too far from the dock. Unlike the remainder of the island, Turtle Cove had more elevation and I noticed some great spots for hiking past the main beach.

The car turned up a steep hill and my back pressed into the seat, watching us climb. When we reached the peak, my jaw gaped. From here I could see almost the entire island; all the sandy beaches, the residential areas full of villas, the palm tree-lined walkways.

"Thank you for bringing me here," I told Joe.

His fingers entwined with mine and he held us back as the car crested the hill and drove back down toward sea level. "No one else I'd rather be with."

When we finally reached the villa Joe had rented, the sun was high in the sky and sweat beaded on my brow as we climbed out of the car. Removing his thin blazer, Joe carried our bags to the front door while I tipped the driver. I could already see his shoulders redden in his tank top, realizing he probably hadn't had a chance to put on sunscreen yet. Being a vampire came with some obvious perks like added speed and strength, but the sun sure liked Joe's kind a little more than the rest of us. It wasn't that he could burn into ashes, as the myths humans had started said, more that he would have a raging tan that would require more aloe vera than the island had in stock.

Thanking the driver, I rushed to Joe with two bags to help him out.

"Now we're talking," Stella said from behind me.

I cast her a sideways glance. "Nice of you to finally show up."

Ignoring me, the ghost pulled her famous vanishing act, reappearing a second later to my right. "Oh, you are going to love this place!"

As she gushed over the villa's exterior, Joe deftly inserted the key into the lock, the metal clicking with a satisfying precision as he turned the handle. With a gentle push, the door glided open, revealing a sight that could rival the most extravagant of architectural spreads. A symphony of modernity greeted us, an open-concept layout that flowed seamlessly from one space to the next, exuding an aura of sophistication straight from the glossy pages of a design magazine.

Every facet of the villa had been meticulously curated, from the sleek marble floors that gleamed under the soft illumination, to the kitchen that beckoned with its state-of-the-art appliances, adorned with delicate bronze accents. It was as if we'd stepped into a world where every element had been crafted with the utmost care and attention to detail, leaving no corner untouched by luxury.

I trailed my fingertips along the smooth silver frame of a generously sized mirror, the reflection casting back the image of a place that seemed untouched by time. "Are we the first to rent this place?" I asked, my voice tinged with curiosity.

Joe shook his head as he dropped our bags onto the elegant bench in the foyer, the weight of his response punctuating the air. "Not at all," he murmured, his gaze sweeping over the immaculate surroundings. "The owner takes great pride in maintaining all of his properties to perfection."

But 'perfection' seemed an understatement as I ventured further into the villa, each step revealing another layer of opulence that surpassed my wildest expectations. Unlike the pristine facade of bright white plaster that greeted us at the entrance, the rear of the villa emerged as a spectacle of glass, a panoramic view of the world beyond captured within its hold.

Shielding my eyes against the sun streaming through the floor-to-ceiling windows, I couldn't help but marvel at the view laid out before me. I pressed a palm against my forehead, allowing my gaze to wander over the expanse of white sands and the shimmering turquoise waters that stretched out to meet the horizon. "Wow," I breathed out. Joe really outdid himself.

"Right?" Joe agreed. "And I'm pretty sure it's a private beach. Though I believe we might share it with the villa next door."

"Same owner?"

Joe nodded, proceeding to walk into the kitchen. He opened the fridge and pulled out a chilled bottle of bubbly, smirking. "Now, how about we celebrate our first day properly?"

After a few glasses of champagne—for me, not for Joe, because vampire—we took a short stroll on the beach before freshening up for dinner. Upon Stella's annoying insistence, I wore a body-hugging silk dress in an emerald green and pinned my hair halfway up with a few vintage diamond barrettes I stole from Gran's jewelry box. Slipping into leather sandals, I carefully made my way down the extremely steep stairs that led from the upstairs bedroom to the main living area. My fingers white-knuckled the railing the whole way down.

What monster designed these?

"That is quite the dress," Joe said from the bottom of the torture staircase.

My cheeks burned with the temperature of the Earth's core. "Thanks. Stella picked it out."

I instantly regretted mentioning the ghost because she appeared out of nowhere with a satisfied look on her cocky face. Stella's abrupt manifestation made me miss the last step. I yelped, sliding down awkwardly and smashing headfirst into Joe's chest. Grumbling, I straightened out and brushed back my loose curls. "Oops," I mumbled.

Lucky for me, Joe was used to my clumsy ways and only grinned before offering his arm for support.

"How far is the restaurant?" I asked.

"That's the best part," Joe replied. "It's a five-minute walk down the beach. Ready to go?"

We slipped out of the sliding doors leading to the beach and took to the sand. The heat of the day was beginning to subside, and I inhaled deeply, relishing in the early evening. To our right, the sound of water lapping the shore offered a comfortable beat to walk to, each swoosh making my feet hop a little. A few seagulls gathered on the shore, picking away at something they'd found in the sand. I rolled my eyes over the beach and the few palm trees lining our path, my heart warming.

My head turned as we passed the villa beside us, the one Joe said had the same owner. It was almost identical to the house we stayed in. I wondered if the two were built at the same time. From this vantage point, I could glimpse directly into the living room. I gulped when I noticed a couple sitting on the beige sofa inside. They were both on their phones and paid no attention to us, so I felt a little better about my spying ways.

It appeared the couple was much more interested in whatever was on their phones than the stunning view right outside their villa. The woman flipped her long brown hair over a bare shoulder, readjusting the straps of her blouse, which had a plunging neckline. Her beige trousers camouflaged into the sofa fabric and drew my attention back to her deeply tanned face. I frowned at her uninterested expression.

Beside her, the man was not much more animated. He scrolled through his phone, pinching the screen and tipping his head back every now and again. Unlike the woman, he was dressed in a stuffy cream suit that looked like it could boil someone alive in this island heat.

The man looked up and his blue eyes caught mine. I averted my gaze instantly, suddenly finding the seagulls that much more intriguing. My eyes stayed glued on the birds until Joe interrupted my thoughts.

"Here we are."

I stopped short at Joe's voice. I was so preoccupied with the couple next door, I completely got lost in thought. When I looked up, my eyes flicked to a row of lit torches lining a cozy walkway to a patio straight out of a fairytale.

Nestled at the water's edge, Beggars Dock emerged as a picturesque seafood haven. The gentle rhythm of waves caressed the weathered wooden deck, where a handful of round tables stood adorned with crisp white tablecloths and vibrant vases of tropical blooms. Stepping inside, we were greeted by a spectacle: a circular bar, aglow with the flicker of countless tea lights, stood as the centerpiece. Its shelves groaned under the weight of innumerable bottles of liquor, a testament to the bar's extravagance. Behind the bar, a sprawling aquarium teemed with life, its azure depths alive with a kaleidoscope of colorful fish. From beneath a meticulously crafted pirate ship sculpture, a sinuous eel slithered forth. This place was nothing short of amazing.

"Welcome to the Beggars Dock," announced an elderly figure, his attire evoking the spirit of a seasoned pirate. Intrigued, I wondered whether a theatrical performance awaited later in the evening.

Sensing my curiosity, the host offered a mischievous grin. "Here, at Beggars Dock, everyone becomes a pirate," he declared, brandishing two eye patches. "Even our esteemed guests."

With a chuckle, we picked up our costumes and followed the host to a table closest to the water. There was a bottle of white wine already chilling on the table when we sat down.

I arched a brow. "Did you call ahead?"

"Guilty as charged," Joe said. "I read online that the lobster is the best on the island."

"Should I order it so you can live vicariously through me?" I teased. "I can get extra butter sauce for effect."

Joe pressed a hand to his chest, pretending to be wounded. It made his tight short-sleeve button up even tighter and I tried to breathe through the pressure building in my gut. "You are an evil sorceress," Joe joked.

"Witch. Not sorceress."

Laughing, Joe perused the menu then looked around. "Weird question, but are we alone?"

"Are you talking about Stella?" I asked. "She's not here. Turns out even Stella Rutherford has boundaries. Who knew?"

Before I could say anything else, Joe leaned over the table and his lips met mine. A dull yearning built up in my chest and my breath caught, savoring the moment. I closed more of the distance between us. No matter how often it happened, I would never get used to being kissed by Joe Brooks. The man was addictive.

When Joe pulled away, I was breathless and red as a bushel of beets. It wasn't long before our server arrived and we ordered our meals; me, the lobster, and Joe, the steak—for show. The night moved along flawlessly and I had to admit, I didn't think of Mom or Hades or the Sisters of the River once. All I wanted was to keep talking to Joe in this sliver of paradise we found ourselves in.

If I didn't know magic existed, tonight would certainly be proof of it.

"When is it going to be enough?"

The sharpness of the voice tore my attention from Joe to a few tables down from ours. In the middle of the dinner rush, a couple appeared to be having a very heated argument. Their arms flailed as they raised their voices louder and I caught a few choice words being exchanged. I narrowed my eyes, leaning over Joe to see clearer.

My heart sank to my sandals.

It was the couple I saw on our walk over here. Our neighbors.

I watched in stupefied horror as the woman picked up her glass of wine and tossed it in the man's face.

Across from me, Joe's jaw slacked, and he worked it hard, trying to think of something to say. But there were no words for what we were witnessing.

Head shaking, the man wiped his face with a napkin and stood up abruptly. The chair fell backward as he rose and the wood slammed into the patio with a loud bang. Everyone stared.

Not bothering to wait for his date, the man tossed a wad of cash on the table and stormed out of the restaurant, his back rigid as he made his way down the beach toward the villas. I wanted to walk over and ask the woman if she was all right but something held me back.

Don't get involved. Leave it alone.

Listening to my inner logic for once, I pressed myself into the chair I sat in and didn't move a muscle. A few minutes later, the woman got up and left. The entire scene put me on edge and I found myself reaching for my glass of wine eagerly.

"Well, that was strange," Joe said.

I nodded. "Very. They live next to us, you know. I saw them on the way here."

"Huh," Joe mused. "Quite the first night out, I'd say."

I couldn't agree more. Despite the sour turn of the evening, I forced myself to forget about what happened and concentrated on Joe. After all, we were here to escape the drama of Orchard Hollow and my messed up life, not dredge more trouble into it. Whatever our neighbors were arguing over, it was none of my business. This week was for me and Joe, and I guessed, Stella.

It was not for spying on neighbors and public fights that left a pit at the base of my stomach.

CHAPTER
5

My sandals, their straps gently swaying with each step, hung loosely from my fingertips, as if reluctant to part ways with the serene atmosphere around us. The soft grains of sand tickled my bare feet, their warmth seeping through every pore, creating a connection with the earth beneath. Alongside me, Joe's hand clasped mine, his touch a comfort I craved. His fingers traced soothing circles on the surface of my palm, each motion sending shivers down my spine.

The flavors of the dinner earlier lingered on my tongue. Now, as we strolled along the shoreline, the rhythmic lullaby of the waves serenaded us, playing a melody that harmonized with the gentleness of the ocean breeze. The sun on the horizon painted the sky in hues of amber and tangerine, and my stomach flipped at the view.

With each step, the sand yielded beneath my feet, its granular texture a delightful sensation that elicited a playful grin. Oyster Bay was a sanctuary, where time seemed to stand still and worries melted away like the receding tide. As evening descended, wrapping us like a cozy little blanket, I couldn't help but marvel at the pure serenity that permeated the air, infusing every moment with a beauty that transcended words.

"Are you getting tired out yet?" Joe asked.

I peeled my gaze from the orange and red line beyond the darkening water to look at him. "Never," I whispered. "I think I needed this more than I realized."

"I could imagine. How are things going with Sylvie?"

I frowned, feeling the weight of the question settle on my shoulders. Despite its apparent simplicity, it resonated with complexities that mirrored the web of my relationship with my mom. How were things with her? It was a question that opened a labyrinth of emotions.

In truth, I found myself grappling with uncertainty. I longed to give Joe a reassuring answer. Yet, honesty compelled me to admit that our journey was far from a straight path toward peace.

The aftermath of her impromptu visit and the harrowing ordeal of solving the mystery behind her friend's murder had certainly nudged us closer together. There was a fragile sense of improvement, a glimmer of hope amid the shadows of our past. But to say that our relationship had blossomed into perfection would be a disservice to reality.

We were navigating through uncharted waters, striving to mend a broken bond. Each step forward was met with hesitation, every moment of closeness tinged with unresolved conflicts. Still, there remained a flicker of determination—a silent promise to keep trying, however daunting the path may be.

And how could it be simple, considering that I didn't think I could ever forgive her for lying to me for all these years? At the end of the day, I could likely forgive the whole 'leaving me to live with Gran while she tried to infiltrate the Sisters of the River.' But not telling me my father was Hades himself and binding my magic on top of it? That was levels of crossing the line that didn't deserve a second chance.

Then again, it wasn't like I went out of my way to stay in touch with her, either.

I grimaced, turning away from Joe and concentrating on the sand. "Still complicated." *To say the least.*

"If I can give some unsolicited advice..."

Stretching my lips, I nodded for Joe to continue.

"Take it from someone who had a terrible relationship with his parents," he said. "The last thing you want is to regret not trying. I don't think I will ever speak to my family again and not a day goes by that a part of me wishes things were different."

An ache formed in my chest. Joe had never given me the details of what happened with his parents; all I knew was they no longer spoke. For some reason, I assumed he was glad not to have a connection to his family, but it appeared I was quite wrong. Maybe it was because he kept his past on a close lock that I didn't press him on it. Or perhaps the fear that I would lose him if I acted like a needy girlfriend.

Whatever it was, I assumed Joe would fill me in when the time was right.

I looked around at the dreamy view before us. What better time than here and now?

Slowing my pace, I dragged Joe down to the sand and we sat facing the water. Our toes stretched out, the rising tide creeping up and licking them with each wave. I peered at Joe's solemn face and my heart broke for him. Who said vampires didn't have a heart?

"You know, if you ever want to talk about it," I said, "I'm a great listener. But no pressure, of course."

Joe turned his head at the same time as I leaned in to kiss his cheek and our noses smashed together. The hit made my eyes water. I jumped back, my fingers massaging the bridge of my nose, where a tingling sensation continued to brew. "Sorry," I said between tears.

Joe laughed. "It wouldn't be a date unless you tried to run me over somehow."

Memories of our first meeting flashed before my mind's eye and I burst into laughter. To think that it wasn't so long ago that I was trying to convince myself that I didn't have feelings for Joe and now, well, now I was definitely falling for the man.

It was petrifying.

"And I promise when I'm ready to share the sordid history of my family," Joe added, "I will." His face scrunched. "Not that it's a particularly interesting topic."

I shot him a glare of disbelief, my lips pouting. "And my mom is much better?"

"Are you kidding? Secret covens? Daughter of Hades? Someone could write a book about you, Piper Addison."

Another laugh bubbled out of me and I slapped Joe's arm, stretching my legs out further. A light breeze kicked up particles of sand, the air around us shifting from day to night. My eyes squinted to see further ahead. We weren't too far from our villa but without any lights, the beach was darker than the rifts I tried not to think about.

Joe had better remember the way back, because my sense of direction was failing quickly. I leaned out to see over his shoulder, my spine curling in relief when I spotted the lights I'd accidentally left on in the living room. At least we had a beacon to guide us home.

The thought made me picture Joe and me as old-time sailors on a yacht and I stifled another giggle. As I turned to face Joe, I noticed the familiar look on his face I had come to crave. *Here we go,* I thought. *Kisses with Joe Brooks on the beach is what you came here for.*

Slowly, Joe leaned in and I inched closer, readjusting my seat so I didn't face plant into the man this time. A gnawing feeling tugged at the rear of my brain and I paused. Joe, noticing my discomfort, asked, "What is it?"

"I'm not sure," I replied. "It feels strange. Like something is—"

"Piper! There you are!"

My teeth knocked together, and I proceeded to grind them furiously. Gaze drifting up a pair of long, semi-sheer gray legs, I locked eyes with my familiar. "Hi, Stella. Perfect timing, as always."

The ghost waved her palm in my face. I desperately fought the urge not to call on my father to drag her sorry behind to the Underworld.

"Oh," Stella said, her brows arched high. "Sorry to bust up the party. There's something you should probably see."

I groaned. "For the millionth time, I am not interested in any more outfit suggestions."

At my side, Joe bristled but stayed quiet. By now, he knew not to come between Stella and me when we were in mid-disagreement. One could lose a limb if they did that. Getting ready to zap my annoying familiar, I called for my magic and held my electric hands high.

"I don't think those will help right now," Stella said, brushing me off. "It's this way."

She pointed a long finger to an off-the-beaten path on the beach that led into a copse of palm trees. Following her gaze, I tried to see what she was motioning to, but all I could make out were shadows cast by the massive leaves and a whole lot of nothing. I tilted my head to the side, my interest peaking. "What are you pointing at?"

Instead of answering, Stella disappeared and reappeared closer to the trees, waving us over.

Frustration bubbled in my belly as I rose to stand. "Stella is here and wants to show us something."

"Cryptic," Joe said.

I couldn't agree more. The ghost was all about the drama and it looked that I couldn't even go on vacation without her antics. Waiting for Joe to jump up, I marched toward the path Stella stood near and followed her into the darkness. Behind me, Joe wrestled with his pants pocket, finally pulling out his cell phone and turning the flashlight on. He tilted his phone higher to illuminate the path.

"This is severely uneventful," I said.

"Just walk faster, please."

Eyes flitting to Joe, I let Stella drag us further down the path until we were deep within the trees. From here, you couldn't see any of the beach at all and even though I knew where it was, save for the sound of the water, I'd never be able to find it. I turned behind me, seeing the same dense trees on the other side.

"Stella, this is creepy," I said. "Someone could easily—"

My words fell away. The light of Joe's phone caught on a shape in the darkness close to Stella's feet. I swallowed, daring myself to get a closer look. As we neared the ghost, more of the light fell on the ground, illuminating the unmistakable shape of feet.

A lump grew in my throat as I realized what we were looking at.

"Is that a?"

I nodded, then reached for Joe's arm to direct it. Raising the flashlight, I fought back a scream as the feet turned into legs which turned into a man's body lying on the ground. The sand had stained the crisp suit fabric he wore, but I knew who it was before I even looked at his face.

Our neighbor. The same guy that stormed out of the restaurant hours ago and left his date alone.

My gaze traveled up his body and landed on his neck. This time, I didn't hold back my scream. Twisted around his thick neck was an orange fishing net. From the look of the man's horrifying expression, I'd say someone used it to strangle him.

"We need to get out of here," Joe said.

He nudged me to move, but I stayed my ground. My eyes continued to scan the body for any sign of life, but there was none. The man was dead. I froze, my attention locking on the dainty gold chain in his hand. I bent down, reaching for it. Joe stopped me before I could do anything stupid.

"Don't touch him," he advised. "The police will not be happy if you disturb the scene."

Of course. You'd think after all my run-ins with

the law, I'd know the protocol by now. I looked up at Joe and Stella, a shiver tripping down my spine. "Well, there goes our perfect getaway."

CHAPTER 6

Bright, blinding lights illuminated the evening sky, casting an eerie glow over the scene below. Police cruisers formed a solemn procession, their red and blue lights flashing in a synchronized dance, while officers in uniform moved with them along the street leading to the beach entrance. The air was thick with tension, punctuated by the distant sound of waves crashing against the shore.

Nestled on the sidelines, I sat next to Joe, our figures silhouetted against the darkness, huddled under a blanket that smelled of coconut sunscreen—a token from one of the officers. Despite its warmth, a chill seemed to seep through the fabric, sending shivers down my spine. Perhaps it was the cool evening breeze that swept in from the ocean, or perhaps it was the unsettling reality of our situation.

We had been stationed here for hours, our stay punctuated by moments of whispered conversation and anxious glances. As the night wore on, the initial sense of urgency began to fade, replaced by a gnawing sense of unease that settled deep within me.

And then there was the body.

A grim reminder of what lurked beneath the surface of our idyllic surroundings and an ominous presence on the beach.

As I sat there, trembling beneath the blanket, I couldn't help but wonder what secrets lay buried beneath the sand. Were there more bodies here? It was a foolish thought and one that I pushed away quickly.

A man in his early fifties with a short, trimmed beard and a flower-print shirt walked the perimeter of the sectioned off crime scene. His pen scribbling in a tiny notebook. He reminded me a lot of a younger version of Sheriff Romero, all business. Around him, a few younger police officers followed his direction as they inspected the body while we waited for the ambulance to arrive. It was uncanny how close the night resembled all the times I stumbled on dead bodies back in Orchard Hollow, except the coroner at home usually didn't take hours to get there.

I wondered if this was the first person to die of unnatural causes in Oyster Bay, which would explain why the procedure was lackluster. Except that couldn't be possible, could it?

Mom did say that I was more likely to be attracted to death because of my magical heritage, but it was beginning to look like I may be more than a magnet for it. What if death followed me?

"Mr. Brooks and Miss Addison?" a deep voice asked.

I looked at the flower shirt, forcing a meek smile. It never reached my eyes. Seeing my discomfort, Joe extended his hand, taking control of the conversation. "Joe and Piper is fine," he said. "Any news on when we can leave? It's our first night here and I must admit, it's been eventful."

Flower Shirt did not appear to care one bit about our stay, nor Joe's extended hand. A scowl formed on my face when I saw Joe retract his arm like he had been burned. What kind of person behaves so carelessly around people who had just been traumatized by what was supposed to be a quiet retreat? The more I thought about it, the more I disliked Flower Shirt. He was nothing like Romero. Our sheriff could be gruff, but at least he had a heart.

"Yes, I understand this is probably very distressing," Flower Shirt said. "I'll try to get you home as soon as possible. You said you're staying at the villas down the beach?"

Joe nodded and opened his mouth to speak, but I beat him to it.

"I'm sorry to interrupt," I said, my voice hiding very little of my growing anger. "But we have been here for hours now and no one has so much as offered us an explanation as to why we need to stay. None of your officers have taken the time to secure the scene. The ambulance is coffee knows where, and as far as I recall, I am yet to see your credentials. Is this standard procedure here?"

Joe tensed next to me, but the corners of his lips twitched. *That's right bucko! Not my first rodeo.*

"Ma'am, I can guarantee you we are following all the proper procedures," Flower Shirt announced. "As for who I am, the name is Hollard Sanders, Lead Detective of Oyster Bay Police. Now, I do have some questions for you two. We can do it here and send you on your way, or you're welcome to follow me to the police station."

The temperature of my body dropped drastically. *Way to go, Piper. You insulted the detective.* The anxiety from the evening must have done a number on me because, with the way I was acting, I wasn't making any friends. Memories of Romero's annoyed face flashed before me. If I wanted to avoid being dragged to the station, I had to play nice. No matter how frustrating the situation was.

I fixed my crooked expression and batted my lashes. "I didn't mean to offend," I told the detective. "It's a lot to handle on vacation, is all."

"I understand, ma'am." *Since when was I a ma'am?* The detective fixed the wrinkled collar of his shirt. "You said you were out for a walk and found the body?"

Joe and I nodded in tandem.

Glancing over his shoulder at the path between the trees, the detective frowned. "Odd place for a walk. A little on the dark side."

The way he looked at us made my cheeks burn. Was this man implying we were doing something a lot more adventurous back there? Uh-uh!

I started to correct him, then quickly realized that admitting how we actually discovered the body would get us locked up immediately. *My ghost familiar led us to it, sir.* I masked my laugh with a cough and faced the detective.

"This is a tad embarrassing," I said. "But I had too much to drink and couldn't make it back in time. If you know what I mean."

"Everyone knows what you mean."

I side glanced to my right to see Stella Rutherford appear beside me. She faked a yawn then said, "You were better off letting him thinking you were getting frisky back there."

Grinding my teeth, I stretched my arm with enough force to shove my hand through Stella's chest. She growled, vanishing with a huff. As she did, a light wind blew past the detective, rustling his curly hair.

"Right," he said, his eyes searching the area briefly. "Did you notice anyone else on the beach this evening?"

My brain raced to play out the evening, but nothing came to mind. Next to me, Joe did the same thing, thinking back through the night before saying, "Not anyone we paid attention to." He scratched his five o'clock shadow, his eyes narrowing. "But the couple was at the restaurant with us earlier. Had a nasty fight, and the fellow stormed out."

The detective's ears perked up.

"Do you know what the fight was about?"

I shook my head. "We didn't want to pry," I told him. "It seemed pretty serious, though. The woman he was with dumped a drink on him right before he left."

"Hmm." The detective stared at us unblinkingly for a few moments before holding up a finger. He stormed off, returning with a tablet that looked like it was made a decade ago. The thing was a brick. When Sanders finally powered it up, I noticed the emblem of the Oyster Bay Police pop up on the screen, followed by a photograph. The detective turned the screen around to face us. "Is this the woman you saw?"

Both of us leaned in and it took me only a second to recognize the woman in the picture. It was definitely her, our neighbor and the one we saw the victim with at the restaurant.

"That's her," I told Sanders. "Who are they?"

"Robert and Carla Atlas. They've been on the island for a few months. Husband is here for work." He winced. "Was."

My body stilled. "They were married? Where is Carla? Shouldn't she be here right now?"

"We can't locate Mrs. Atlas," Sanders replied.

"As in, she's in the wind?" I pried. "That's pretty suspicious, don't you think?"

A flash of annoyance ran over the detective's face and he bit his lower lip, studying me with the gaze of someone trying to hold his tongue. "Please leave us to do the police work here, Miss Addison. I can assure you that no one is *in the wind,* as you so delicately put it."

From inside the trees, someone called the detective's name, and he held up a finger again, telling us to stay put. The tablet was still clutched in my cold hands and I took the time to inspect the couple. They were so polished and appeared to be so happy that it was hard to picture them as the same people we saw fighting earlier. It was even harder to picture Robert dead, but I tried not to think about the body lying twenty feet from us.

Instead, I focused on Carla. She stood with her back straight, leaning slightly into Robert as he hugged her into him with one arm. Her dark brown eyes twinkled in the camera flash and her hair was sleekly tied back into an impressive updo. Both were dressed in black-tie attire, and I wondered if they were on their way to a gala. The Atlases struck me as the type of couple that went to events like that.

My eyes caught on the enormous diamond earrings in Carla's ears.

I nudged Joe. "Those probably cost more than my house."

"I suppose they were well off."

An idea sparked in the back of my mind. I scanned the trees for any sign of the detective. When the coast was clear, I pulled out my cellphone and aimed it at the tablet screen.

"What are you doing?" Joe asked.

I shrugged, snapping a quick photo. "In case we need it later."

Joe didn't say anything else, but I could see the wheels turning in his head. He was thinking the same thing I was. Something was amiss with our neighbors, and considering how close we were to the crime scene,

I wasn't taking any chances. My experience with the police in Orchard Hollow hardened me and though I was certain things were different here on the island, I couldn't help but think they were also very much the same.

My stomach twisted into knots. The last thing I wanted was to get caught up in another murder investigation, especially while I was supposed to be relaxing. In the corner of my eye, I spotted a stretcher being wheeled out of the trees, a body bag atop it.

"Ambulance arrived," Joe said. "We can finally go home and forget all about this."

I didn't have the heart to tell him that forgetting about the night was no longer on the table. Something told me whatever had happened here wasn't over yet. Where was Carla tonight? I looked past Joe toward the two villas sitting stoic against the night sky.

Why wasn't she here grieving for her dead husband?

CHAPTER 7

W aking up in Oyster Bay was complete bliss. I had never done yoga, but I assumed this was how one must feel after a particularly long session. Any nerves I might have had were gone after a night on the plushy mattress in the air-conditioned villa. The farmhouse didn't have central air, so the only way to cool down in the summer months was to open all the windows and hope for the best. It worked decently for the most part, but there were plenty of days where my clothes clung to me in sweaty creases.

Well, not here. Even my unruly hair hung down in perfect red ringlets. Oyster Bay agreed with me.

I stretched my lazy limbs and looked out the wide

upper balcony doors. From this vantage point, the ocean felt like it was directly on the other side of the wall and even though I couldn't hear it with the doors closed, I could imagine the sound of the waves clear as day. A flock of seagulls flew overhead, their wings flapping. The sun was already high in the sky and a panic rose within me. How long did I sleep?

I turned to the empty side of the bed.

And where was Joe?

Reaching over to the nightstand for my phone, I was about to call him when I spotted a piece of paper on his pillow. Carefully, I brought it up to my face, my eyes focusing slowly on the writing.

"Be back soon. Went to get breakfast."

I pressed the note to my chest with a smile.

"He's a keeper," Stella said.

My breath caught in my chest and I sucked it in, choking on it. Crumpling the note in my hand, I scrambled to clear my airways and ended up coughing up a lung instead. Tears streamed down my face as I fought for air. I collapsed into the headboard, heaving, when I finally managed to regain it.

Perching on the edge of the bed, the ghost had zero concern for the daylights she scared out of me. "Very attractive," Stella drawled.

"You scared the latte out of me!" I shrieked, tossing the balled up note at her.

Stella dodged it without breaking a sweat. Could ghosts sweat? I shook my head. *Stay on course.* Eyeing her suspiciously, I asked, "Where did you go last night? I didn't see you when we got home?"

"I'm on vacation, Piper. Let me have my privacy, please." Shrugging, she got up and brushed invisible lint from her transparent tennis skirt. "Come downstairs. The water is beautiful right now."

Cocooning myself in a thin robe, I slipped into a pair of beach sandals, grabbed my phone, and made my way down. When I reached the landing, I spotted Stella reclining on one of the tanning chairs in the backyard, her eyes closed and her chin tilted up to soak in the sunshine. I wondered if she could feel the warmth of it, my smile dropping when I realized how foolish that was. Stella was dead; she couldn't feel anything ever again.

As I poured myself a morning coffee, I tried not to think about how much my heart broke for my familiar. Being dead seriously stunk.

Sliding the doors open, I scooted into the second chair and took my first sip of some of the best coffee I'd ever had. It was no Coco-latte, but it was dark and with a kick and exactly what I needed. Savoring the taste, I kept my eyes on the bright blue water so I didn't have to see Stella fake tan and end up crying.

Suddenly, my phone vibrated in my pocket. I

opened the incoming text message with a grimace. "Ugh!"

"What happened?" Stella asked. She made a show of looking my way, but kept her eyes closed.

"I asked Cilia to keep an eye on the farmhouse while I was gone and look at what she sent me."

Turning the phone around, I shoved it in Stella's disinterested face and waited until she gazed at the screen. Her eyes widened in mock-horror. She inspected the picture once more, then rolled her baby-blues and returned her attention to tanning. "I told you to get rid of the monster."

I bit my bottom lip and zoomed in on Harry Houdini lying on his back in my kitchen with a dozen half-eaten bagels scattered around him. The furry rascal was fast asleep, and I swore I could see a little bit of drool dripping from the side of his mouth. Behind him, the cupboard he got into was destroyed.

"I need to tell the mailman to check his truck better," I told Stella. "Harry is hitching rides with him like it's a cab."

As I turned my attention back to the phone, a loud bang broke the silence of the beach. Stella and I jumped up in unison. Our eyes met, and we followed the trajectory of the sound past our villa to the one next door. It was eerily quiet now that we weren't speaking, or breathing, and the muscles of my legs tightened as I rose to sit higher in the chair. Another bang shot toward us and I gasped.

Next to me, Stella pressed her index finger to her lips. "Zip it."

I froze. Sucking in a slow breath, I placed my cup on the side of the lounger and stood up. My head turned right and left, but the beach was completely deserted. If someone was next door, they didn't come out this way. Yet.

Moving as quietly as I could, I chucked off my sandals and motioned for Stella to check out the villa next door. It was probably Carla knocking things around, but I didn't want to risk it. Frankly, the loud noises I heard sounded a little too frantic, and I had an uncomfortable feeling in my chest. What if Carla needed help?

Inching closer to the rear of the neighboring villa, I gripped my phone tightly while I waited for Stella to report back. The ghost took her freaking time. I didn't know what she was doing next door, but by the time she returned, my shoulders slouched and my feet burned from the heat of the sand.

"What did you find?" I asked.

"No one home."

My expression twisted. "What was that noise, then?"

The ghost vanished without answering my question. I waited a bit longer and when it was clear she wasn't returning, I groaned and walked toward the Atlas villa. As I approached the big glass doors leading from the beach inside, the color drained from my face. They were wide open. From the looks of them, they'd been left ajar for some time since sand had gathered into a pile in the living room.

Glancing over my shoulder for Joe, who was still gone, I straightened my spine and walked into the villa.

The first thing I noticed was the absolute mess of the place. Chairs were overturned, cupboards were left wide open, there was a pile of shredded papers in one corner of the living room. I even spotted a broken planter lying sideways on the floor. On the wall to my right were two large holes. I had to take a closer look to make sure they weren't bullet holes. They weren't. It appeared something used to hang here that wasn't there anymore. I did one more circle around the villa, my pulse rising.

What happened here?

My hair flew sideways as Stella manifested next to me. "Someone did a number on this place, huh?"

"Sure did," I agreed.

Careful not to disturb anything further in case the police needed it for evidence, I ventured deeper into the villa. My eyes scanned every nook and cranny and

I filled my fingers with my magic in case someone was still here. As I walked, I realized how similar the layout of the Atlas villa was to ours. It was almost an identical match, but mirrored. I stopped in front of the staircase leading to the second level and let out a low whistle. Even the killer stairs were the same.

Settling my trembling hands, I gripped the railing and pushed my way up.

"Carla?" I whisper-yelled when my bare foot landed on the top stair.

No answer. *Seriously, where is this woman?* If my husband died, I'd be at home in a wreck, but the villa was completely abandoned. I wasn't sure what to make of it. Originally, I assumed Carla probably killed her husband and ran off, but now that I saw their place, I wasn't so convinced. Someone was definitely after something in here. Could it have been Carla that turned the place upside down? It was a possibility, but one I doubted. For some reason, I worried about the woman's well-being.

Then again, I'd been known to be wrong and Carla was probably off hiding somewhere and washing her husband's blood off her hands. Metaphorically, of course. The man was strangled.

The marble floor was cool against my burning skin and I bit the inside of my cheek as I briskly walked along the upper floor. Much like the downstairs, this level was destroyed. If I had to guess, I'd say the place was burglarized, but it was hard to tell with so much junk in the way. I stepped over a shattered blue vase on my way into an unlocked bedroom. Immediately, my gaze landed on the oil painting of a sailboat leaning against the wall. Directly above it was a safe, and it was busted open.

"Why would anyone rob the place and leave that behind?"

I followed Stella's pointed finger to the safe and the stack of cash there. Inching closer, my brow scrunched when I saw the wad of money that was resting on top of a black velvet jewelry box. Using the corner of my robe, I pushed the money out of the way and opened the box. Inside lay a diamond tennis neck-lace that, if it was real, was worth more than this entire villa. Behind the box sat three more identical cases that had similar expensive jewelry tucked in them.

I gaped at the safe. "This doesn't make any sense."

Leaving the safe, I walked toward the bedroom window and peered outside. The view was much the same as the one I woke up to this morning, except here I could see right into the backyard of our villa. The thought made shivers trip down my spine. If the person responsible for what happened here looked out the window, they could have seen me. I had no clue why, but the idea made me want to flee the Atlas residence and crawl into a dark, deep hole.

Not wanting to spend any more time in what I was now sure was an active crime scene, I turned to leave. Behind me, the sun shone brightly into the room and a sparkle on the ceiling fan caught my attention. As the fan took another turn around, I saw it again.

"Huh," I whispered to Stella, who was more interested in the diamonds than anything I had to say.

Realizing my partner in crime had mentally checked out, I walked to the switch on the wall and turned the fan off, then dragged a nearby chair to the center of the room so I could climb up. My legs wobbled as I stretched out high enough to reach the blade of the fan. Patting the smooth metal surface, I ran my hand over the fan until I hit a ridge. "Got you!" I yelped and yanked the object hard enough to free it.

The chair danced under my weight and I clambered off it, falling clumsily half on the bed and half on the floor. My hip groaned as hit into the wooden base of the bed and I winced from residual pain when I tried to get up. If there was ever an eye-opening moment that I needed to exercise more, this was it.

One good part of the entire fiasco was that I finally had Stella's full attention. She towered over me—all legs and bones—and pointed to the shiny object in my grip. "What's that?"

I held up the key I found taped to the fan. "Looks like a key. Why do you think it was up there?"

"No clue," Stella said with a shrug. "But if I were you, I'd get out of here."

"You think they might come back?"

Stella floated into the hallway and peered toward the stairs. "I don't think they'd risk it, considering the cops have shown up."

She was right. I was so busy with the fan I didn't hear the sirens outside or the voices echoing from the front of the house. Legs pumping, I rushed down the stairs, careful not to trip the entire way down. I reached the sliding doors right as the front door swung open and the police poured in. Moving at the speed of light, I slipped outside and bolted for our villa, tripping over the lounger as I scrambled to get inside.

My chest heaved with short, rapid breaths and I was covered in sweat; a combination of adrenaline and island weather. Sitting down on the cream sectional in our living room, I leaned on a pillow and uncurled my shaking fingers.

The key was still there.

CHAPTER 8

"Anything on that website?" I turned the key over in my hand. "Or what these numbers might mean?"

Sitting across from me at the marble-clad island, Joe typed on his laptop, his eyes narrowing in concentration. He scrolled down the page he'd opened and his posture slumped. "Nothing here. The sequence of numbers looks similar, but they aren't coordinates."

"And they don't match the lock boxes at the airport, either."

After I filled Joe in on what I discovered next door, we polished off our breakfast without so much as chewing and got to work. Joe must have been bitten by the mystery bug because he only mentioned how dangerous it was to go next door alone once. Either that or he needed the distraction. Was Joe bored on this trip already? I shook off the thought. Sure, Oyster Bay wasn't the romantic getaway we planned yet, but who could get bored after the night we had?

I looked at the key again. And now this...

"I don't understand why someone would hide a key that doesn't appear to lead anywhere," Joe said. "Perhaps it was a mistake."

My brow quirked. "Who tapes a key to a ceiling fan by mistake?"

Shrugging, Joe returned his focus to the laptop while I racked my brain for fresh ideas. The bronze key lay idle in my hands, its weight a gnawing pressure. I took a sip of the cold coffee in my cup and sighed. Iced lattes made everything better. As I lowered the glass, a chill ran down my spine and I instinctively closed my fingers over the key, relaxing them when Stella appeared beside me.

"Any luck tracking down the bank?" the ghost asked.

I choked on my drink. "Bank?"

"For the key," Stella said. Seeing my confused expression, she added, "The safety deposit box the key opens. At a bank. You do know that's what it's for, right?"

If stupidity had a face, it would be mine. Well,

mine and Joe's because neither of us thought of a bank safety deposit box, even though now that Stella mentioned it, it made a lot of sense. After the revelation, it took us almost no time to track the key to Stanford Royal Bank. According to their website, the bank was favored by travelers due to its very strict privacy regulations.

I pocketed the key and slipped my feet into a worn-out pair of leather sandals, then looked at Joe. "Feel like going for a ride?"

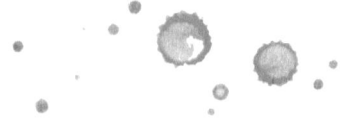

Stanford Royal Bank stood amidst the hustle and bustle of a major tourist area, a modest structure standing stoically just a fifteen-minute drive from our villa. Nestled on the corner of a bustling street, its unassuming facade belied the financial hub within. Adjacent to the bank, a tourist shop called to me with its flamboyant displays of trinkets, from shimmering keychains to rustic straw hats, while across the way, a florist's shop stood silent and shuttered.

With a firm grip, Joe ushered us through the weighty wooden door, the reverberation echoing in the air as it sealed shut behind us. The interior greeted us with a space as empty as the depths of a vault, dotted only by a sparse scattering of patrons, patiently queuing for service. My gaze wandered, tracing the line of closed doors flanking the main teller area, each one a tantalizing mystery, perhaps concealing the coveted safety deposit boxes.

As we advanced toward the information desk, a door creaked open, releasing a wave of urgency into the main area. A stern-suited gentleman emerged, his hurried steps echoing through the space as he made a beeline for the exit. In his wake trailed a younger counterpart, frantically scribbling on a pad of paper, a silent messenger of urgent to do's.

"Hello, there. How may I assist you today?" the woman behind the reception desk asked, her voice warm and friendly amidst the bank's somber ambiance.

I stepped around Joe, flashing my pearly whites at her. Either the woman was made of stone or she couldn't care less about my positive attitude because she barely acknowledged my existence. Her eyes rolled over Joe and I felt heat fill my stomach.

Clearing my throat, I pressed my elbows on the round desk she sat behind and leaned in. "We'd like to speak to someone about getting a safety deposit box."

"Certainly," the woman said. She readjusted her

gold frames and shook out the mane of wavy hair on her head. I couldn't be certain, but I could swear that when she looked at Joe again, her eyes glimmered. "I'll see if there's an account manager that can come speak to you."

Continuing to ignore me, she typed something into the computer behind the desk and pressed a button on her headset. Normally, I wouldn't be bothered by the blatant disregard for my existence, but for some reason, I had to fight to stop myself from snapping at her. My teeth ground against each other even as Joe wrapped an arm around my waist and pulled me into him, a gesture that earned us a scowl from the receptionist.

Pressing another button on her headset, she let her gaze drift from Joe to me. "Mr. Young will be with you in a moment."

It took five minutes for a short, stocky man in a tailored black suit to greet us. Mr. Young's well-manicured hand shook mine, then Joe's, and he led us toward a seating area near the teller desks, motioning for us to sit down. Joe seemed as comfortable as ever, his background as a lawyer making him well used to dealing with stuffy people in even stuffier places. I, however, managed to somehow perch on the edge of the seat and slowly slide toward the floor as the conversation went on. Sweat beaded on brow despite the intense air conditioning in the bank as I battled gravity.

"It's a pleasure to meet you..."

"Mr. and Mrs. Brooks," Joe said.

My eyes bulged out of their sockets and my butt slid down a little further. I knew Joe was only playing the part, attempting to make it more plausible that we were here to rent one of their boxes. It was definitely easier to tell the manager that we were a married couple than to explain how only one of us needed the box. The best way to attract less attention was to simplify the lie, and I knew in my heart that was why he spared the man from knowing my last name. And yet those stupid butterflies fluttered non-stop in my stomach at the sound of the implication.

"Piper?" Joe asked, his face a mask of concern.

There was a good chance I turned blue from the loss of oxygen to my brain. Shaking off the intrusive thoughts, I straightened out and forced a pathetic grin. "Sorry about that," I said sheepishly. "I was lost in thought for a moment. As—" I paused before I called Joe my husband "—Joe said, we're hoping to rent a safety deposit box from you. Is that a service you provide, Mr. Young?"

"But, of course," the manager said eagerly. "And Thelonious is fine. What style of box are you looking to rent?"

My fingers grazed the edges of the key in my pocket. I wondered what box it belonged to, but without any prior knowledge of how any of this worked, I didn't have the slightest idea. As I opened my mouth to say something that would probably give us away, a flicker by one of the closed doors near to us caught my eye. I turned my head, my jaw clamping shut as a figure came into view. *Really? Now?*

Fighting to keep my face blank, I watched as the ghost of an older man appeared in front of me. His eyes were milky, and he had so many wrinkles that he resembled a newborn Shar Pei puppy. My gaze trailed over his old-fashioned suit and the gold name tag attached to his blazer. Simon Shrodecker - Bank Manager.

The ghost, Simon, turned up his hand to wave me over before disappearing behind the door.

My jaw unhinged.

"Everything all right, Mrs. Brooks?"

Shuddering, I closed my gaping mouth and said, "Do you have a bathroom I could use?" Adding, "I'm sure Joe can fill you in on what we need. I'll be right back."

By the time I reached the door Simon ducked into, my hands were lit up like Christmas trees and I had to shove them under my blouse to keep from lighting the bank up with my magic. Glancing behind me, I waited until Thelonious turned away and the other few tellers were busy before testing the lock. The handle jiggled but didn't give. I grunted. Keeping one eye on my surroundings, I pushed a sliver of my magic out. It burst from my fingers, singeing the metal with a zap. When I tried the handle this time, it twisted to open.

Not wasting time, I slipped into the room and closed the door quickly behind me. It was darker here than the rest of the bank, and it took a moment for my eyes to adjust. I looked around at the narrow, tight space I occupied. There wasn't one piece of furniture in the room and it was more of a corridor than an office. At the farthest side, another door beckoned me forward. I rushed toward it, repeating my trick with the handle to get it to open.

Stepping into another room, I gasped as I walked right through Simon's ghost body. Unlike Stella, he didn't make a fuss and only chuckled in response.

My hands shot up apologetically. "I'm so sorry!"

Simon waved me off, but didn't say a word.

Odd.

"Why did you call me over?" I asked the ghost. "Do you need help?"

Simon shook his head negatively and pointed behind me. It was starting to look like there was more he and Stella didn't share; Simon couldn't say a word. Following his ancient, trembling finger, I turned and took in the wall behind me. There were small compartments taking up the entirety of the wall with keyholes in their centers. Under each keyhole was a gold plate similar to Simon's name tag, with numbers etched into it.

I stumbled a step backward. "Are these safety deposit boxes?"

Simon nodded.

Score one for Piper!

Pulling out the key I found, I studied the numbers, my eyes watering from the low light. It took a second, but I was able to match them to a box at the bottom of the middle row and when I tried the key, it worked without a hitch. My heart raced in my chest as I pulled out the deposit box from the wall. A creak pierced the silence of the room as I ripped it open and I winced, praying no one heard me in here. Moving as fast as I could manage, I pulled up the lid and peered inside. The box was empty save for a few pieces of paper.

Unfolding them, I inspected the contents better, my brain working overtime. "Are these blueprints?"

Next to me, Simon shrugged.

As far as help went, he wasn't all that great as a partner. I leafed through the blueprints a few times, still not knowing why they were locked up. Before putting everything back, I snapped a few photos on my phone and turned to leave. "Thanks for the help,

Simon," I told the ghost as I pulled myself through the narrow opening of the door.

In the bank, things were as I left them. I breathed out in relief and made my way back to Joe, who was keeping Thelonious—what an obnoxious name—quite busy. He was describing our uneventful plane ride in excruciating detail by the time I reached the two.

"Oh, hey, honey," Joe said. His eyes searched mine for any hints of where I ran off to, but I was a locked vault. "Thelonious said he'd love to give us a tour if we have the time."

"Actually, we have that thing soon," I objected. "With Carla Atlas."

"You two know the Atlases?" the bank manager asked.

I studied his shocked expression in glee. I hit a nerve.

Noticing me glaring, Thelonious pressed his lips together tightly and tipped his chin. "It's a shame what happened to Robert. He was one of our top clients."

So it was Robert who rented out the deposit box... I was jumping to conclusions, but I liked the odds of my theory. Who else would tape the key to the fan if not the man who lived there? But why hide it from his wife? The details didn't sit right with me.

"How do you know them?" Thelonious asked.

Joe stood up to stand next to me, his arm sliding

around my waist. "We rent the villa next door. News travels fast around here, I see. We only heard about what happened recently."

"Small island," Thelonious said calmly. "Please offer my condolences to Carla. And watch out for Mr. Harding."

My brow creased. "The villa owner?"

"A rightful snake, that one," Thelonious said. It was shocking to see the professional act drop. I supposed the bank manager really didn't like our landlord. "The last time Robert was here, he mentioned Harding was trying to raise the rates on him. The Atlases had been in that villa for almost a year! A deceitful way to conduct business, if you ask me."

Realizing he'd spoken too much, the bank manager straightened his already pristine tie and cleared his throat. "Are you sure I can't give you a proper tour of our fine establishment?"

Not after that gossip session, buddy.

"We really should be going," I said. "Oh, Carla mentioned a safety deposit box that her husband rented here. She asked if she could stop in to gather its contents. I let her know we would check since we were going to be here, anyway."

The color drained from Thelonious's face and he looked everywhere but at me. His hands reached into his pockets and he pulled out a card, handing it to Joe.

"I'm afraid I don't know what you mean, Mrs. Brooks. But if you decide you'd like that tour after all, do give me a call."

With that, he turned on his heels and strode away, leaving me and Joe by ourselves in the middle of the bank. We exchanged confused glances. "Strange guy," Joe said.

I nodded and started for the exit. As I walked out of the bank, I searched for Thelonious, who was pretending to busy himself with a stack of papers at the reception desk. Strange man, indeed. Even stranger that he blatantly lied.

CHAPTER 9

In the sunlit kitchen of the villa, the aroma of sizzling shrimps danced through the air, infusing every corner with a devouring fragrance. Joe, adorned in a crisp white apron, moved effortlessly, his hands dancing as he cooked. The pan crackled as he expertly tossed the shrimps, each one coated in a medley of exotic spices that made my stomach growl in anticipation.

As I settled onto one of the polished brass-legged bar chairs, my senses exploded. The butter bubbled in the pan, releasing its rich aroma. My mouth watered.

With every flick of the wrist, Joe seemed to weave a spell, transforming simple ingredients into a feast fit for royalty. Though no magic was involved, of course. At least not the paranormal kind.

As I watched in awe, I couldn't help but marvel at the alchemy taking place before me. In Joe's hands, food wasn't only for eating—it was a masterpiece. And as our lunch took shape, I couldn't help but feel grateful for the opportunity to witness his culinary magic firsthand.

My lips closed around the rim of the wineglass and I took a slow sip, savoring the chardonnay. "Where did you learn how to cook?"

"One of my clients was a chef," Joe said. "He ran into some trouble back in the day and I traded my legal services for cooking lessons." He flipped the pan in one smooth motion, sending the shrimp flying high. "I think I got the better end of the deal."

I laughed. "Unless the chef is in a jail cell, I think you both got what you needed."

"Excellent point," Joe said, winking. "So, you want to tell me why we ran out of the bank like the place was on fire? Let me guess. Stella?"

The pan hissed and Joe removed it from the stove, set it aside, and began to work on the sauce. Sitting on the counter beside him was a steaming bowl of pasta awaiting its toppings. I licked my lips, looking around the villa. No sign of Stella yet. Now that I thought about it, I hadn't seen the ghost since our trip to the neighbors. I wondered what she was getting up to on the island and if she enjoyed the change of scenery. One thing I knew about Stella was her love of travel. She once told me that she and Arthur used to go on four trips a year. Sure, they could afford it, but I wouldn't leave my home that often no matter how much money I had. That was the big difference between us. I was a homebody and Stella was a globe trotter. That, amongst many other things.

I took another sip of wine and tossed a fresh slice of cucumber into my mouth.

"Those are for the salad."

Eyes glued to Joe's, I slowly picked up another slice and chewed it quickly. "Not Stella," I answered his previous question, hoping he didn't catch me eating more of the garnishes. "But there was another ghost at the bank. A manager, I think. Looked like he died a very long time ago."

"Oh?" Joe's eyebrows hiked up into his hairline. "Your powers kicked in?"

"Sort of. The guy couldn't talk, which could have been a him problem, but it could be my powers aren't strong enough yet."

At the stove, Joe scratched the rear of his neck and I tried to ignore the sensation that his muscled arms left in my belly. "You hear Stella fine."

"Sure," I said with a shrug. "She's my familiar, so I think that has a lot to do with it."

"What about Isabella?"

I touched my chin in thought. "True. You just reminded me I have to call Mom later. She wanted details of the trip, though I doubt she's expecting what I'm going to tell her." I paused to snatch a slice of green pepper when Joe wasn't looking. "Anyhow, I did find something interesting at the bank. A set of blueprints."

The shrimps went into a pan of sauce and the smell of garlic filled the air. My stomach growled so loud I had to fake a cough to muzzle the sound. Behind me, the open double doors let in the breeze of the afternoon and I could hear the waves lap the shore. Aside from what happened to Robert last night, it was turning out to be a pretty wonderful vacation. Or at least it would have been if I could get the blueprints and what they could mean out of my head.

"Do you think they were important?" Joe asked.

I cleared my racing thoughts. "Definitely," I said. "Why else would Robert have rented a safety deposit box for them? It was the only thing inside. Maybe you can take a look later and see if you can figure out what they were for."

"You stole them?"

A ladle dropped on the floor, the sound of metal

on tile pinging through the kitchen like nails on a chalkboard.

"Of course, not!" I exclaimed. "I took a photo with my phone. Why do you think Thelonious lied about Robert renting a box at their bank?"

"I don't know. Could be company policy," Joe mused.

Somehow, I didn't think that was the case. Call me paranoid, but there was a part of me that knew Thelonious lied. His eyes darted nervously, his voice faltering just slightly at key moments. What bothered me most was that I didn't know why. Did Robert ask him not to mention it? What was so important about those blueprints that they required so much secrecy? The weight of unanswered questions hung heavy in the air, like a thick fog obscuring the truth.

Between the bank manager's lie and the hidden key, the stupid papers were better hidden than a national treasure. Each piece of the puzzle seemed to lead to another dead end, frustratingly out of reach. It was as if someone had meticulously created a maze, and I was trapped in the center, struggling to find my way out.

I frowned, wishing there was a way to suss out the truth without ruining the rest of our stay here. As Joe plated our food, a thought flashed before me like a bolt of lightning in a stormy sky. Not quite a full-fledged idea, but a glimmer of possibility amidst the chaos. It twitched on the edges of my consciousness, daring me to grasp it despite the risks involved. That is to say, the thought I had definitely tracked on brand for me — reckless, impulsive, and utterly irresistible.

The mischievous glimmer in my eye caught Joe's attention, and he groaned, running his fingers through his short hair. "Oh, no. I know that look. What are you plotting?"

"Nothing too wild, I promise," I said. "You know how Thelonious mentioned that Robert and our landlord had a disagreement over rent?"

Joe nodded with hesitation.

"And didn't you hear the air conditioning groaning and banging around last night?"

"I didn't."

I reached over the bar and playfully smacked his arm.

Chuckling under his breath, Joe pushed a plate over my way and handed me a fork. I inhaled the delicious goodness of the meal, waiting before I devoured it like a rabid animal. To my surprise, Joe didn't start eating. Instead, his eyes narrowed on me and he leaned in so close our foreheads touched. "You're planning to have the landlord over here as soon as you can manage, aren't you?"

"Guilty..."

Finally, Joe stabbed a fork into an unsuspecting shrimp and offered it to me.

"Well, if you're going to be tricking men into spilling their guts about a murder," Joe said, "you can't do it on an empty stomach."

Sweet coffee bean. My boyfriend was hard not to fall in love with sometimes.

CHAPTER 10

Collin Harding had a wide mouth and thick-rimmed glasses that made him appear very unassuming. Which was why I had my haunches up as soon as he stepped through the threshold of the villa. The rental owner greeted us warmly and, to our surprise, brought a bottle of wine that I assumed cost a fortune as a welcome gift. Joe thought it was a lovely gesture.

I, on the other hand, had less than positive feedback. From my unfortunate experience with unsavory individuals, those that were the sweetest often had the most to hide.

After leaving the wine on the counter, we huddled in the kitchen and made awkward small talk for a good ten minutes while I jumped out of my skin silently. When Collin finally asked to see the air conditioning unit upstairs, I all but leaped for joy. Which was how I now found myself biting my nails down to the bone while he stood on a ladder and tinkered with a unit that I knew had nothing wrong with it.

"And you said there was a noise?"

I cringed. "Yes. Like a congested cough."

Across from me, Joe arched one eyebrow and pressed his lips together. His eyes crinkled at the corners as he worked hard to contain his laugh. I couldn't blame him. My lies were ridiculous.

"A cough, huh?" Collin asked, seemingly unaware of the silliness. "Just the one time, or did you hear it again?"

"Through the night," I said. The show must go on...

My head stayed glued to one spot, so I didn't have to look at Joe because one glance his way and the jig would be up. I could barely keep up with the story as it was. Biting my bottom lip, I worked to recall what else I told Collin on the phone so I could keep the facts together, but all I could think of was the million questions I wanted to ask him. How well did you know Robert Atlas? Was it true that you tried to gouge him for more rent? Did you, by any chance, happen to strangle him with a fishing net?

You know, the usual conversation starters.

The ladder shook as Collin climbed down to stand beside me. He shoved a screwdriver into his tool belt, a fancy leather one that looked expensive, and gave the air conditioner another glance before turning to me. "It seems to be fine now," he said. "If you hear the noise again, see if you can record it so I know what to look for. But there doesn't appear to be any damage to the unit, and it's cooling the place fine."

A finger shot up in the air to prove the point. I smiled awkwardly and watched Collin head for the stairs to leave. Before he reached them, I nudged Joe in the ribs. *A little help here.*

Shaking his head, he caught up to Collin at the landing.

"Since we have you here, think I can bother you for a list of places to visit?" he asked. "We've seen all the suggestions on the island's tourist site but were hoping for a more genuine experience."

Collin's eyes sparked with interest.

"Why, of course!" the man explained. "I can definitely suggest some off-the-beaten-path destinations. There are quite a few."

A bead of sweat rolled down my back, even though we were standing directly in front of the air conditioner. "How about we go downstairs? I can whip up iced coffees and you can tell us all about this gorgeous island of yours."

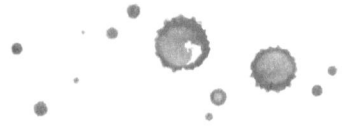

Two rounds of Coco-lattes later and Collin was still going on about Oyster Bay. It was starting to look like our landlord was even more of a chatter box than Rory, an impossible feat at best. As he recounted every detail of the island's history, my mind drifted back to Orchard Hollow. I checked in with Rory earlier this morning and from the sounds of it, she had things handled. Cilia even spared a few people from the hotel to help out with the rush hour shifts. As far as I could tell, Bean Me Up was under control. Or at least still standing, which was all I could ask for after leaving a teenager to run the place in my absence. I didn't even want to think about the mess the back office would be when I returned. Rory sometimes used it to practice her spellwork, and she wasn't the neatest witch in town.

Images of potions exploding flashed in my mind and I shivered, pushing past my racing thoughts to focus on the two men in front of me.

"One place you absolutely have to visit is the

iguana sanctuary off Turtle Cove," Collin said. "There is a pond that houses a large population of them."

Again with the lizards... I pushed my empty glass away. "What's with all the iguanas here? They seem to be a big deal."

"The iguanas are a protected species on the island," Collin replied. "Over the years, they've become somewhat of a mascot and the tourists love seeing them. Have you encountered any in the back yet?"

My eyes bulged. I looked past Collin to the back of the villa that opened up to the beach. I hadn't seen any creatures crawling around yet and the thought there might be iguanas in the backyard unsettled me. Not that I had anything against them, but I had enough trouble with Harry Houdini and from the way Collin described the animals, they sounded an awful lot like the raccoon. Feisty and always stealing food.

Head shaking, I scanned the backyard once more to be safe. "We haven't seen any yet."

"Oh, you should definitely make it out to Turtle Cove. Come to think of it, the guy next door worked for the developers hoping to build there."

"Robert Atlas?"

Collin's face blanched. He stabbed the straw of his drink in and out of the cup, refusing to look up. "You've met? A shame what happened." His shoulders hiked up to touch his earlobes. "I can promise you the island is very safe, in case you were spooked by the incident."

Joe's thigh pressed against mine under the table and we exchanged quick glances. Studying Collin, I tried to gauge the man's intentions toward the Atlases but so far, he didn't appear to have a very close relationship with either of them. He also didn't strike me as someone who would kill a renter over a money dispute. My jaw tensed and I squirmed in my seat before asking, "Do you know if Robert had any enemies on the island? At work?" Trying not to come off like I was snooping, I added, "It would put my mind at ease to know it wasn't a random act."

"Piper is right," Joe agreed. "If it was premeditated, at least we'd sleep better knowing whoever killed the guy wasn't coming back."

"Trust me, there is no need to worry! This area you're in is basically heaven on earth," Collin said. I noted the lowered conviction in his voice. "But you do have a point. I'm sure it wasn't an isolated accident."

My ears heated. "How so?"

The question put Collin on edge. I watched his eyes crease as he narrowed them to inspect me. *Shoot. I messed it up already.* Coming to my rescue, Joe flashed a row of perfect white teeth and said, "Piper is somewhat of a detective savant. Loves a good mystery." He wiggled his eyebrows mischievously.

By some small miracle, it worked.

"Well, you didn't hear it from me," Collin said, excitement in his voice. "But Greenfield Industries, Robert's employer, was known to be a bit of a real estate shark on the island. They take over land right, left, and center, without a care for anyone else. I wouldn't be surprised if their list of enemies is a mile high."

Trying my best not to make eyeballs at Joe and give away our plan to keep Collin talking, I stood from the table and poured another glass of iced coffee from the carafe. While I added a dollop of whipped cream to my drink, taking my sweet time to perfect the swirl, Joe kept Collin occupied. He slid a bowl of freshly cut mango his way and handed the man a fork, saying, "Sounds like a land tycoon. What are they building over at Turtle Cove, anyhow?"

"Another obnoxious resort, from what I heard from Robert," Collin answered. "Like the island needs more of those. If you ask me, what we need are smaller, less obtrusive businesses to bring in lovely folk like you two. Not giant monstrosities taking away everyone else's views of the water."

The spoon slipped from my fingers and clinked the marble tabletop. I winced, picking it up quickly and wiping the whipped cream stain off before Collin noticed. The last thing I wanted was for our landlord to see me destroy the place. He might try to raise our rent, too. Chuckling at my lame joke, I picked up my glass and took a long sip as I thought about what Collin had said. If he was right and Greenfield Industries wasn't well liked on the island, it stood to reason someone might want to hurt Robert. The blueprints we found in the safety deposit box came to mind and I struggled to remember what they looked like. I vaguely recalled a drawing of a large pool and buildings. A lot of buildings. Could the blueprints have been for the resort the company was working on?

"What did Robert do for Greenfield Industries?" I asked.

Collin's brow furrowed in concentration. He tapped an untrimmed nail against the side of his glass, his eyes narrowing slightly. "You know, I'm not sure. He was one of the architects on the job, I believe." His lips puckered. "You'd have to ask Carla." Mouth quirking into a grin, he added, "Or Monica."

"Monica?"

There was a long pause between us that filled the villa with an air of awkwardness strong enough to make me shiver. It was obvious Collin regretted his slip of the tongue but there was nothing to do about it now, we all heard him drop the name and judging by

Joe's face, he was as eager to find out why this Monica character was important as I was. How many women did Robert have around? I felt awful for thinking ill of the idea, but so far, Collin wasn't painting the best picture of the man.

That, combined with what Joe and I witnessed at the restaurant, was giving me all the heebie jeebies.

I grabbed my glass and rejoined the men at the table, sliding into the seat and folding my arms before me. When Collin was still quiet as a mouse, I cleared my throat lightly to urge him on.

The landlord huffed out a breath between clenched teeth and faced me head on. "I probably shouldn't have said anything," he started. *And yet here we are...* "Monica Boatman is Robert's boss's wife. I'd seen her around the villa quite a lot lately. To be honest, I suspected something was going on between her and Robert, considering how often she visited. Not that I was prying."

Yeah, right!

I battled the urge to roll my eyes.

"That said, Monica was always here whenever I stopped by as of late," he explained. "Poor Carla. I really felt for the woman."

The way he said Carla's name made me think he might have felt more for her than he was letting on. Was there perhaps more than empathy in Collin's heart for the widow? It was hard to tell from one sentence, but I couldn't help shake the thought.

I paused, catching on the other meaning in Collin's words. "Why were you by so often? Was something wrong with the place next door?"

"You could say that again!" he exclaimed. "When the Atlases first rented the villa, it was meant to be a short stay. Well, it had been months and, based on the resort in the works, it would be much longer. I tried to reason with Robert about the rental fee since I was considerably undercharging, but he wouldn't hear of it. We had quite the fallout for a bit there."

Beside me, Joe leaned in closer to Collin, his eyes storming. "Did you two settle things in the end? Before the unfortunate event."

"Sure did," Collin said. "I got to tell you, I would hate to have our fight be the last thing to go down with a tenant." He glanced at the watch on his wrist. "Well, I should get going. Sorry for blabbing on so much. If that air conditioner gives you any more trouble, you give me a call."

As Collin said his goodbyes and stepped out, I couldn't help but replay the conversation in my head. If Robert was having an affair as the landlord suggested and Carla found out, that could be reason enough to kill her husband. Especially when you paired this new information with what we witnessed.

The Atlases did not strike me as a couple in love. But could things have been bad enough for Carla to resort to murder?

I had no idea.

About to ask Joe what he thought, I walked toward where he hovered in the front foyer, noticing him pocketing his cellphone. He turned around with a bewildered look on his face that quickly turned to frustration.

"What's wrong?" I asked as I approached.

Joe rubbed his temples until there were two red spots on his skin. "That was the local police station. They want us to stop by at our earliest convenience."

"Why?"

Shrugging, Joe opened the front door and waited until I put my sandals on to step out. "They didn't say," he replied. "But it sounded urgent."

My heart beat wildly in my chest as I made the short walk from the front door to our rental car. Between the police, the murder, and the iguanas, the trip was a lot less relaxing than I expected it to be...

CHAPTER 11

The police station loomed on a hilltop a thirty-minute drive from our villa. With the way the island was laid out, we could cover the entirety of it in just over an hour, and I tried to think of the ride as a sightseeing opportunity. My mind raced while Joe parked, the sights I was excited to see quickly replaced by an inner dread I couldn't shake.

One more police visit to add to my list.

Parking at the small lot at the base of the hill, Joe opened the passenger door and extended his hand to help me out. Normally, I'd have made a joke about being an independent modern woman, but my head was elsewhere. So I took his hand without a second thought and grudgingly climbed out of the car.

"We'll be in and out," Joe promised.

I really wanted to believe him, but my experience with cops had proved otherwise. Not to mention that the detective on the case did not appear to be all that pleased with me after I badgered him about Carla's whereabouts. In my defense, the widow was yet to show her face next door, so as far as I was concerned, she was guilty as sin.

Readjusting my low ponytail, I followed Joe up the steep driveway to the front door of the station. "Let's get it over with and grab drinks, okay?"

"It's a deal."

A gust of wind tickled my ear. I slowed my steps to give Stella a chance to keep up. At this point, her constant popping in and out of our living realm was becoming so much of a habit that it barely bothered me. Surely the ghost had better things to do than stick by my side all the time and while I was grateful for the privacy, I missed her snooty behind when she wasn't around. A second after I felt her arrive, she appeared at my side, her body almost entirely solid.

I eyed her up and down. "The tropical weather looks good on you."

"You should take my lead and take a break while you're here," Stella suggested. "Get a tan, let your hair loose, do some sightseeing." Her large eyes narrowed to slits as she trained them on the station's entrance. "The kind that doesn't include this place. Seriously, Piper, are you able to leave well enough alone for once?"

I rolled my eyes. "Not my choice this time. The detective wants to see us," I explained, then turned to Joe. "Stella thinks we're wasting our vacation."

"Stella *knows* you're wasting it," the ghost corrected.

Next to me, Joe dipped his chin and chuckled. "I couldn't agree with you more, Stella," he told my familiar. "But after this, it's all fun and play. No matter how many bodies Piper trips over."

Smacking his arm, I turned my attention to the ghost. While these two were busy mocking me, I had an idea that might help speed all of this along. Stella was right, I did want to enjoy the island more, but I also knew from personal experience that murder cases took time to solve. If we could offer some help to move the ball forward, how could I say no?

Lips pouting, I stared at Stella until I had her full attention. "Any chance you could scope someone out for me?"

"Piper, no," Joe protested.

I pretended not to hear him. "Can you see what you can find out on a Monica Boatman? She's married to Robert's boss and apparently there may have been something going on between the two. Could you follow her and see what you come up with?"

"You want me to stalk someone on vacation?" Stella asked at the same time that Joe said, "Don't ask her to spy."

Are these two on a make-life-difficult-for-Piper team? Come on guys! Work with me here!

Brushing past both of them, I stomped to the station. When I reached the entrance, I turned to look at them over my shoulder. "The faster we can get to the bottom of what happened to Robert, the faster we can get back to tan lines and margaritas. You didn't honestly think the police would leave us alone? We were the only witnesses."

I wasn't sure which one of the two I was speaking to, but it seemed to do the trick. Joe huffed out a frustrated breath and rubbed his forehead, his expression that of surrender. A few steps from him, Stella inspected her arm with a frown.

"I can't believe you're making me stop my sunbathing to play peeping Tom," she said.

"You can't tan anyway," I told her. "So you'll do it?"

Turning on her heels, the ghost flipped her long ponytail at me and started to vanish. Before she disappeared, she hissed out, "Fine. You owe me big time." Then she was gone.

I waited until I was sure Stella wasn't coming back before reaching for the door handle. Now that we had a plan, the weight on my shoulders lessened slightly and the dread I felt earlier began to subside. Opening the door, I walked into the station with Joe behind me and headed for the front desk. My stomach growled, and I grimaced. Somehow, I had the feeling that we wouldn't make it to drinks for quite some time.

The Oyster Bay downtown police station was a stark contrast to the one back at home. For starters, it was a bright and cheerful space with a skylight over the main waiting area and indoor palm trees scattered around, making the place look like a mall. Then there was the absence of local drunks slouched in the chairs; a staple in Orchard Hollow. I met Joe's gaze as we trekked behind a uniformed officer as she led us to a private room, mouthing "fancy" behind her back.

Joe chuckled with a shrug.

The officer opened a door—one that wasn't locked —and gestured for us to step inside. Walking through the threshold, I expected to see wall-to-wall concrete with a single depressing desk in the center. My jaw hit the floor when I took in the room we were dropped off in.

"Is this for real?" I asked, taking in the bright white

walls and leather sofa in the room. There was another palm tree near the large window on the opposite side of the sofa and a polished aluminum coffee table with a few local magazines on a tray atop it.

"Nicer than my apartment," Joe answered.

For a second, my mind drifted. I started thinking about the fact that in the time I'd known him, I had never set foot at Joe's place. We always got together in the farmhouse or in one of our businesses and, for the first time, it struck me as odd that he never invited me over. Perhaps it was a vampire thing. They were usually quite private. Still, we were currently on vacation together so clearly I had been upgraded from casual fling status.

I made a mental note to ask Joe about it when we returned home.

"Apologies for the wait," a familiar voice said behind us.

I turned around to watch Detective Sanders enter the room. He closed the frosted glass door behind him and pulled up a chair from the corner of the room to sit across the couch. Motioning for us to sit, he said, "I had a few more questions and figured it'd be easier to ask them here."

Easier or more intimidating? I wasn't so sure which one he meant.

"How long will this take?" Joe asked.

The detective raised his hands in surrender. "Not long at all," he said. "Now, if you don't mind."

He pointed to the couch again and grudgingly, we obeyed, sitting down close together. Joe's palm rested on my thigh and he gave it a little squeeze of encouragement, which helped release the pressure building in my body. On the plus side, if we had to make a run for it for some reason, we both had our magic to help us out. Somehow, the thought was less comforting than I wished it was. An image of my magic malfunctioning and blowing the detective to smithereens flashed before my eyes.

I closed them tightly, pushing the thought away.

"I wanted to know if you heard anything unusual next door yesterday," the detective asked. "Early morning?"

He must be talking about the break-in. Shaking my head, I forced a pathetic smile. "Nothing out of the ordinary. It's been very quiet over there."

"Right. How about today?"

"Are you asking if we've heard the wife return?" Joe asked.

The detective didn't have to answer. It was written plain as day on his face that Joe had guessed correctly. *So... Carla was still in the wind. Interesting.* My brow creased. I folded my hands in my lap, facing the detective. "Don't you find it suspicious that Robert's wife hasn't shown up? I mean, her husband was killed. You'd think she'd make an appearance." Leaning in across the coffee table, I pressed my hands to the metal, my eyes never leaving Sanders. "If you ask me, Carla Atlas is looking mighty guilty."

Though I couldn't be certain, I sensed the detective was holding back, telling me what he truly thought of my theory. The creases at the corners of his eyes deepened and his shirt—a parrot pattern this time —stretched over his taught chest as he rolled his shoulders. Outside the room, someone walked by the door whistling an upbeat tune. Another reminder of how different the police force was on the island.

"While I don't disagree with you on how it appears," the detective finally said, "the time of death doesn't line up."

Next to me, Joe's face darkened. "What does that mean?"

"We have recently discovered that Mr. Atlas was killed hours before we originally thought. Carla was on the phone with her sister in Canada during that time. We have her phone records to prove it."

"She didn't do it?"

Color me speechless.

The detective gave me the slightest nod. "Correct. As a matter of fact, now that we have ruled her out, her disappearance is being treated as a missing person case. Which is why it is crucial that you let us know if you hear anything next door."

Goosebumps trickled down my skin and a shiver ripped through my spine. Was he saying what I thought he was saying? My head spun as I collected my wildly running thoughts. "Are you implying that the same person who killed Robert may have taken Carla?"

"I am not implying anything," Sanders said. "I am simply asking you to keep an eye out. If it's no trouble, of course."

After we agreed, the detective asked us about our plans for the remainder of the week before handing Joe his card with a cellphone number on it. As he walked us out, he mentioned that we should give him a call if we see anything odd or if Carla ends up returning. Somehow, I doubted the woman would be back. Whatever happened to the Atlases was bigger than what we were seeing, of that, I was sure.

Trembling, I followed Joe outside, heading for the car. I was still full of nerves when I climbed into the passenger seat, so when Stella popped her head between Joe and me, I shrieked.

"Hi, Stella," Joe said calmly, pulling the car out of the parking lot.

I rubbed my eyes furiously. "Now is not a good time for your scares," I told the ghost.

"You'll change your tune when you hear what I found out."

Sitting up straight, I turned toward my familiar. My pulse sped up and my heart raced in my chest, eagerness filling my stomach. "You found Monica?"

"I sure did," Stella said. "She was acting odd, so I followed her."

"Odd how?"

The ghost pouted her oversized lips. "Oh, you know. Strange. Like she knew she was being watched."

"Where did she go?"

"That's the weird part," Stella replied. "I trailed her as far as that little isle off the coast but lost track of her there. A relief, if you ask me. There were way too many green monsters there for my liking."

Green monsters? What was she talking about? My head swarmed as the realization of where Stella referred to hit me. "You saw her near Turtle Cove," I whispered. "The iguana sanctuary is right there."

"What was that?" Joe asked.

I pretended that what I said wasn't important. As Joe veered the car down the sharp turns off the road, I suggested we eat in instead of going out. After all, we had a perfectly wonderful view back at the villa and this way we could go swimming right after drinks. Joe seemed pleased with the idea, so when I asked if he wouldn't mind dropping me off to pick up the food, he was more than happy to oblige. I could already see the excitement of a romantic lunch on the beach swirling in his mind.

A sliver of guilt gnawed at the back of my brain and I tamped it down. Joe would have to forgive me for what I was about to do. The plan formulated in my mind, and my lips stretched. After all, if I was going to ambush Monica on Turtle Cove, I'd have better luck of going alone.

CHAPTER 12

The cab pulled up in front of a rickety old loading dock. I bit the inside of my cheek as I climbed out, wondering if I'd made a mistake. After Joe left to pick up the food, I bolted out the door, Stella on my heels. It took almost no time to hail a cab, and we were at the dock for Turtle Cove in less than ten minutes. On the way here, I asked the driver if there were many turtles on the isle and he shrugged, saying only, "Not anymore."

As I neared the ticket booth for the boat to take me over, I wondered what exactly he meant.

"Return trip for one?" the woman at the counter asked.

I lowered my sunglasses to look past her at the

tiny boat tied off at the dock. There were already a dozen passengers on board and I could hear the captain explaining the history of the isle over the crashing sound of the ocean waves. "Yes, please," I answered and handed her a bill before I changed my mind.

"See you on the other side," Stella said, vanishing.

By the decrepit state of the boat I was about to load into, I wasn't sure we'd even make it across. I kept my doubts to myself and joined the couple ahead of me as they hoisted themselves into what I could easily describe as an oversized dingy. For a boat so tiny, we made it over to Turtle Cove in record time and I was relieved that I was only seasick for half of the fifteen-minute trip.

When I climbed out, I vaguely heard the captain note the return times. Staring at the white sand and bright blue water that lay still as a bathtub, my breath escaped me. Even without the turtles, this place was magical. To my right, a quaint bar, and restaurant took up a portion of the beach. I watched in amusement as a server carried a carefully balanced tray of drinks to a couple lounging in the ocean. Without so much as faltering, he placed the tray onto the one-legged table stabbed into the ocean sand and waded out, moving to the next table over.

Once I was done, I'd have to bring Joe back to the

isle. I didn't think either of us had ever had drinks at a water table before.

The rest of the passengers I shared the boat with had already picked their spots on the beach. Some brought their own chairs and umbrellas, while others purchased sets from the bar. I noticed a few couples stray away from the main area and dart into the large grouping of palm trees that formed a small forest at the top of the hill.

"Here for the views or the iguanas?"

I twirled around, kicking up sand in the process. Before me stood the same server I saw delivering drinks before, a flute of champagne in his hand. He extended his arm to hand me the drink, and I took it with a smile. "Scoping the place out to see if my boyfriend would like to come back later," I said. It was the closest thing to the truth I could manage.

"Ah, in that case, I will leave you to your sleuthing," the server said. "Most people come for the beach, but if you're up for a hike, the pond is right up that path."

He pointed to the trees I saw people disappear beyond earlier.

"Thank you for the tip. What do I owe you for the champagne?"

The server shook his hand, turning to leave. "Nothing at all," he said over his shoulder. "Think of it as a welcome gift. If you do return with your man, come find me. I'll make sure you two have the best table on the beach."

Thanking him again, I took a few more sips of the champagne and turned around to see the rest of the isle. From this spot, I could pretty much see its entire layout considering how small Turtle Cove was. Laughter exploded from one of the tables in the ocean and I grinned, my forehead glistening from the heat of the sun above me. Once I brought Joe back here, he would have to forgive me for ditching him today. Surely no one could stay mad in a place such as this.

I finished the champagne and set the glass down on an empty table near the bar, then got ready to hike it into the trees as the server suggested. I didn't know where Stella went, but I figured she would show up if I was heading in the wrong direction, if only to point out how off base I was. One would think the vacation would put a pause on her incessant attitude, but that clearly wasn't the case.

Even paradise couldn't change Stella Rutherford.

"Stop flirting and get over here."

And there she is... I frowned at the ghost who now stood under the shade of a massive tree. "First, I wasn't flirting. Second, maybe try smiling for a change. More bees with honey and whatnot."

"I'm allergic," Stella retorted.

"To honey or bees?"

She smirked. "To you," the ghost said. "Now let's go before she leaves."

Stella's sheer body glitched, and she re-materialized a few feet away, close to the dense tree line. She waved her hand impatiently, and I had to jog to catch up with her. Giving the gorgeous beach one last glance, I sped up and vanished into the small jungle covering one side of the isle. My feet padded softly as I maneuvered the wild terrain. Roots and rocks marked an off-beaten path that led us further up to the tip of the hill I saw from the boat. My leg muscles worked overtime to stay steady. I prayed to the coffee gods that I didn't twist an ankle before I reached whatever spot Stella led us to.

A low hanging palm tree leaf came out of nowhere, smacking me across the face. I sputtered. "How much further?"

"Don't be such a baby," Stella said. "We're almost there."

Her form glitched, and she reappeared next to a slight opening to the right the path we walked. Checking behind me for tourists, I rushed after Stella, catching her right before she vanished from view. My arm was getting sliced apart by palm leaves and I was about to tell the ghost off for leading me into the middle of an actual freaking jungle when the trees opened up in front of me. Mouth gaping, I glared at the place Stella brought me to with glee.

"This is unreal," I said.

Before me was a pond large enough to be a lake back home. The color of the water was nothing short of a tourist brochure, and there was a small waterfall in the distance, spilling over a cliff lined in palm trees and greenery. Around the pond, large boulders created a barrier upon which hundreds of iguanas basked in the sun that streamed from above. I caught one little guy scratching his back against a fallen coconut and laughed.

Ah, now I get their appeal. The iguanas were actually pretty adorable.

The area we stood in didn't appear to be heavily populated, and I wondered if many people visited this part of Turtle Cove. If it was me, it'd be the first place I'd go to if not for the waterfall, then to see the sweet little guys that lived here. But there was no one else here except me, and Stella if you counted dead people. My eyes traveled to the rough terrain under my feet. There were a few sets of footprints scattered here and there, and what looked like bicycle tracks leading deeper into the jungle. But no people. Odd.

"She went through there," Stella said.

I followed her finger as she pointed past the waterfall toward what appeared to be more jungle. "Really? Doesn't look like much."

As I spoke, the trees parted and a lone figure emerged. I jumped backward to avoid being seen and my neck smacked into some greenery. Something wet dripped down my shirt. I tried not to think about what it could be. Instead, I focused on the woman emerging from behind the waterfall.

It was hard to make her out in detail from this far away, but I could tell she was beautiful. Her long legs cut through the long grass with ease and she held the poise of a mythical warrior queen. I felt instantly invisible as I watched the woman, Monica Boatman, tie up her long, wavy hair into an effortless top bun. Despite the heat, her makeup was flawless, and she didn't even glisten, whereas I was melting like a witch in a storybook who had water dumped on her.

Near to me, Stella said, "Now that's how you should dress on vacation."

I ignored her, settling my nerves and getting ready to confront Monica. Time to do what I came here to do so I could return to the villa and salvage my relationship. More so, it would be great to bring a lead to the police so they could stop hauling us in for questions. The irony that I was taking time away from vacationing with Joe to question a suspect and possible killer was not lost on me, but I was already here and Monica was so near.

My racing mind would probably stop pushing for answers if I did this.

I watched her slice through the trees with ease, making her way toward where I was standing. As she neared me, my heart sped up and my chest rose up and down with quick and shallow breaths. I filled my lungs and stepped into her path seconds before she passed by my hiding spot.

Expectantly, I overshot my landing and our heads collided with a bang.

"Ouch!" Monica yelped.

I rubbed the growing red spot on my forehead. "I'm so sorry! I didn't see you there."

The woman took a stuttering step backward to put some distance between us. Her eyes narrowed on me and there was a brief look of panic behind them that vanished instantly. Her odd reaction quickly turned around and she welcomed me with a wide grin. Even her teeth were perfect; two sparkling rows of white that belonged in a toothpaste commercial.

"It was probably my fault," she said. "My head was elsewhere."

I waved my hand at the waterfall. "I'm not surprised. The view here is definitely distracting."

Monica looked puzzled, as though I said something strange. She shook her head and rolled her shoulders, stretching out to her full height. I had to tilt my head up to look at her as she towered over me. "Right," she said, still a bit dazed. "Well, enjoy the hike. If you stick around until noon, you can see them feed the devils."

She started to move past me and my heart leaped up into my throat. I had to think of a way to keep her from leaving, something that wouldn't make it so obvious that I was a creepy stalker. My mouth dried up. I swallowed what little saliva I could, the heat of the island suddenly getting to me.

"Oh, yes," I said, feigning excitement. "My neighbor told me about that. The company he works for is building a resort here, so he gave me the scoop of the land."

A foot from me, Monica stopped in her tracks. Her back grew rigid and the muscles in her long legs tensed.

"Hook, line, and sinker," Stella whispered in my ear.

I brushed a hand next to her face, pretending to be shooing away a fly. As I did, Monica spun on her heels to face me, her skin slightly ashen. "Who is your neighbor?"

"Robert," I said, watching for her reaction. "Robert Atlas."

Some of Monica's confidence faded before me just as Stella said, "Got her."

"You knew Robert?" she asked.

I wiped the sweat from my forehead and avoided her eyes when I lied. "Sure did. We're renting the villa next to him and his wife."

"Did you—" Monica stopped talking. "Never mind."

"You're losing her..." Stella sing-songed.

Thinking quickly, I shifted my weight and leaned closer to the woman. This time, she didn't double back as I whispered, "Were you going to mention what happened?" When Monica nodded, I said, "It's all right. Tragic what happened, but we didn't know Robert all that well. Though it sounds like you knew him."

"I did, actually. He worked for my husband."

My fake surprised face could have used some work, but it was the best I could do on short notice. I pressed a hand to my chest, my jaw gaping. "What a small world!" I exclaimed. Stella motioned for me to tone it down with her palm and I turned away from her so as not to break character. One thing Mom taught me was that if you were caught mid-act, you stuck the landing. "What was the name of the company? Greenfield, something or other, I believe."

"Greenfield Industries," Monica said.

"Right! That was it." I smiled. "You said your husband owns it? Must be quite successful to be building a resort."

Eyes darting to the pond, then back to me again, Monica's back stood ramrod straight as she crossed her arms. The silk tank she wore didn't even crease in the process and I worked not to look down at my own outfit that was likely covered in sweat and dirt by now. Her golden gaze landed on me with so much intensity, I almost buckled back. "He does all right," she said. "But it's only money. What matters in the end is love. The only thing that matters."

The diamond bracelet and matching necklace Monica wore told me her husband did more than all right. Why downplay how well-off they were? Most people she knew that had money didn't pretend to hide it and considering how exceptionally well Monica was dressed, she'd have to know how ridiculous pretending otherwise appeared. Her behavior was beyond strange.

"Very true," I said, trying to find common ground with the woman. "Love is king."

She chuckled, but it came off bitter and cold. "Sometimes," Monica whispered. "When you can help who you fall in love with."

Double strange.

Unsure where this was going, I knew my only way

to get her to give me any useful information was to shock it out of her. I had to do something drastic or this trip would have been for nothing. I matched the woman's stoic stance, folding my arms over my chest. "You must be Monica, then," I said. "Our landlord mentioned seeing Robert's boss's wife next door often."

Standing next to Monica now, Stella's eyes widened. She mouthed, "What are you doing?"

I didn't respond. Not only because I would look unhinged if I started talking to myself, but mostly because I really had no clue what it was I was doing. My plan was to get Monica riled up enough to slip up and tell me the truth, but the woman was all walls and sharp angles. I should have known better than to try to outsmart a real-estate mogul's wife. Based on how Collin described Greenfield Industries, the two were probably not all that well liked on the island.

"Whatever that man told you is a lie," Monica said, her expression set on fire. "And if you speak to him again, you can tell him I don't appreciate the implications he's making. And that my husband won't either."

Now we're talking. It wasn't the reaction I thought I'd get, but at least it was something. I widened my stance. "I'm sorry," I said quickly. "I didn't mean to offend you. It's just that what happened to Robert was so shocking. I can't get it out of my head. Who would do something so awful? And in this paradise? I thought if you were around the area often, you may have seen something. Anything to help catch whoever killed him."

Whatever I said made Monica's demeanor change entirely. It was as though her haunches went up as soon as she heard me openly discuss Robert's murder. Her gaze darted around us and the curve of her spine vanished, making her appear to be more rigid than the trees we stood beside. Her fingers grazed her collarbone and the sparkling necklace hanging there.

Taking one step forward, she pushed her face close to mine. "I don't know who you are or what you're doing, but you should stop. Leave what happened to Robert alone," she hissed. "Whoever got to him is dangerous. You should back off before you find that out for yourself."

With that, she twirled around and marched down the path toward the main beach, disappearing from my view. Next to me, Stella let out a low whistle.

"That was something else," she said. "She knows something."

I was about to tell her I agreed when my phone buzzed. Looking at the screen, my stomach turned, and a knot formed in my throat. "Shoot," I said.

"Everything good?" Stella asked.

I shook my head and took off toward the beach, hoping not to run into Monica again. The next boat going back to the mainland was due any moment, and I didn't want to be trapped here much longer. Especially not when Joe was back at our empty villa with lunch and, judging by his text, was very upset.

As the sun rose over the horizon, casting a warm glow over the tropical island, I trudged through the dense foliage with Stella at my side.

"This island is remarkable, despite what happened," I said, brushing a stray lock of hair away from my face as we navigated through the lush jungle. It wasn't far from the main beach now. "But I can't shake the feeling that we're missing something."

Stella nodded solemnly, her translucent form shimmering in the light streaming through the palms.

The sound of rustling leaves nearby caught us off guard. With a cautious glance exchanged between us, we crept closer, our senses on high alert. To our surprise, we stumbled upon a serene clearing bordered by a small pond similar to the one we just left. This one was also full of lazy, chubby iguanas.

"Well, I'll be," I murmured, my eyes widening in amusement. "Looks like this place is full of iguana spas."

As if on cue, one particularly bold iguana lifted its head and regarded me with a beady gaze, its tongue flicking in and out as if sizing me up. I held up two hands in surrender, a smile on my lips. Suddenly, the hands at my sides rippled with magic, a blue electric shock coursing through me. I cursed, shaking it off.

Huge mistake.

The magic shot out from my hands and zapped at the rocks surrounding the pond, causing the iguanas to perk up in confusion. In a flash of chaos, the once-docile reptiles began to mimic my every move, wiggling their tails and blinking their eyes as if coming out of a stupor. A few ran over to me, their bodies slinking between my legs and making me trip. I landed on my butt with a thud.

"Stella! Do something!" I yelped as an iguana began to scale my body.

The ghost floated toward me, but her presence only made the reptiles more restless and they scurried faster, their little feet scratching my skin. I shrieked.

"Get off her, you weasels!" a voice yelled from inside the foliage.

My eyes widened as a head of lettuce rolled out from in between the trees, followed by a second. The iguanas perked up their heads, their eyes following the food. In an instant, they rushed away from me and attacked the lettuce, their nails clicking away on the ground.

The server from earlier extended his hand to help

me up. "Only thing to get them to back off," he explained.

I thanked him, cheeks red with embarrassment.

"Did you get lost?"

I looked around, blinking fast. "Looks like it. I was trying to make the ferry and found this place instead. Is that the way to the beach?"

"Sure is," he replied. "Come on, I'll walk with you. The boat just docked. If we hurry, you won't be stuck here for another hour."

Moving my bruised behind, I followed the server as he expertly led me through the trees and back to civilization. Behind me, the snapping of teeth echoed through the dense foliage as the iguanas finished off their food. I couldn't help but smile. They reminded me so much of Harry Houdini. In my pocket, my phone buzzed. I didn't have to look to know who it was. *Best get back to Joe before he calls in the cavalry.*

CHAPTER 13

"You should have asked me to come with you," Joe said, his head shaking.

I leaned back on the outdoor lounger, scanning his face intently. The creases on his forehead had all evened out, and he didn't look as upset as he did when I came back from Turtle Cove. If anything, he seemed worried, which was, all things considered, much worse. I got so wrapped in my usual act-first-think-later mentality that I didn't take into consideration how scared Joe would be to return and find me gone. Especially with a killer on the loose.

A killer I thought I was chasing.

I was in serious need of a therapy session.

Toes scraping the hot tile, I retied my loose bun for

the twentieth time and bit the inside of my cheek. Joe continued to watch the ocean as it came in to shore, the tide pulling it in and out like a pendulum. I reached out across the space between our loungers and intertwined my fingers with his. "I'm really sorry," I said. "I wasn't thinking. Sometimes I get so obsessed with getting answers that I forget there is an entire world around me."

"You could have been hurt," Joe said, his green eyes finally landing on me.

"I know. I just..." Thinking for a second, I tried to find the right words to explain. "My history with men is not great. I'm not used to being with someone that is present and it's taking me a bit of time to get used to it. I promise it wasn't out of maliciousness. Maybe Stella is right and I am too used to being on my own to make for a good girlfriend."

Joe frowned. "You tell Stella she's wrong next time she shows up," he said. "You make a perfect girlfriend. Except for when you have my heart racing so you can chase down leads."

"So you forgive me?"

"Sure," Joe said. "But next time, please wait for me. You know, you're not the only one who's curious about what happened. And if this vacation turns into a race to find out, I'd like to be in on the action."

My chest swelled, and I grinned like a fool. "Are you saying you want to know what I found out?"

With the slightest tip of his chin, Joe nodded and I burst at the seams. Since my familiar ran off to enjoy her vacation right after we left Turtle Cove, I had been dying to share every detail of what I uncovered. At first, I was disappointed with not getting anything out of Monica or being any closer to finding out who killed Robert. But the boat ride back had my mind going a mile a minute. Something about the open ocean and the pull of the waves did a number on my brain and I was able to read between all the lines of what Monica said.

"Okay, so at first I thought Monica killed Robert out of jealousy," I told Joe. "Or to cover up their affair as Collin suggested. But then I talked to the woman, and she didn't strike me as someone who would do that. That and she was not very pleased with the rumors our landlord was spreading."

Joe rubbed the nape of his neck slowly, the fingers of his free hand still holding mine. "Is it possible she's lying? If I were having an affair, I'd want to keep it a secret."

"I'm going to brush over that visual for my mental health," I said. "And no, I think she was telling the truth. I got the notion that her husband was not exactly the best person. I can't say why, but the way she spoke of him sounded almost as though she was scared of the man."

"You don't think—"

"That Monica's husband agreed with Collin's theory and killed Robert?" I asked. "It's possible."

My body tensed and I dropped Joe's hand, wriggling in the lounger so I could sit on its edge. The waves brushed over the sandy beach and the sound of the palm tree leaves moving in the wind above our heads made me not want to sit still. For most people, lounging with the view of crystal-clear water and the smell of coconut sunscreen in the air had a relaxing effect. Me, on the other hand, all I wanted was to move, move, move.

I rested my elbows on my thighs and put my chin into my palms, looking up at Joe. "Is your laptop handy?"

"It's in the bedroom. Want me to get it?"

I nodded. "If you don't mind. I'd like to see what we can find out about Greenfield Industries and Monica's husband."

"Say no more."

While Joe set up his laptop on the rear deck, I gathered our supplies for the research session. A large pot of coffee, a loaded snack tray, and sparkling wine for dessert. I figured since I was forcing the man to play detective on our romantic getaway, I could at least make it as pleasurable as possible. At least visually since all that stuff was for me. Not that Joe seemed to mind. He wasn't kidding when he said he wanted to help. When I stepped out with the tray of goodies, he already had seven tabs open and was taking notes on a notepad Collin left for us in a welcome basket.

Armed with drinks and food, we started a digital quest, scouring the labyrinth of the internet for morsels of information on Greenfield Industries and its owner, Fallon Boatman. According to the web, Greenfield Industries had carved out its niche over the span of a decade, evolving from humble beginnings into a formidable player in the business. Reports suggested that the company's coffers had swelled significantly over the years, with millions of dollars finding their way into Fallon's pockets, a testament to his shrewd dealings in real estate.

It seemed Fallon possessed an innate talent for identifying lucrative opportunities before they became mainstream, positioning himself as a visionary in the cutthroat world of property development. He was hailed as a modern-day pioneer, credited with trans-forming overlooked parcels of land into bustling centers of commerce. One article called him a "land shark," a fitting title that encapsulated his relentless pursuit of money.

From our search, it became evident that once

Fallon sank his teeth into a project, he clung to it tenaciously, not letting go until he turned a profit. His reputation preceded him, sometimes not in the most positive way.

"Hey, look at this," Joe said, moving the laptop on the small round table so I could see better.

I leaned into the screen, my neck craning and my eyes narrowed to slits. "What am I looking at?"

"The blueprints for the resort he's building on the island. Or the ones Greenfield has up on their website."

Letting out a low whistle, I zoomed in on the image and scrolled left and right. "It's massive. How many pools is that?"

"Twelve," Joe replied. "But does it seem off to you?"

"How so?"

Holding up a finger, he stood up and went into the villa, returning moments later with my cellphone. He handed it over, saying, "Can you pull up the picture of the project blueprints you found in Robert's safety deposit box?"

I keyed in my code and flicked through the gallery until I found the image. Putting it up to the screen, my brow creased, and a lump formed in the base of my throat. I looked from the photo to Joe. "It's not the same site."

"Not by a mile," Joe agreed.

"Why would Robert have these blueprints hidden away then? And if it's not the same location as the one Greenfield is advertising, what would they be using this site for? It obviously isn't for the resort." My eyebrows hiked into my hairline. "You know, when I was on Turtle Cove, there were a lot of iguanas. We're talking hundreds. I think most people go there to see them."

Confusion laced through Joe's features as he said, "Sorry, I'm not following what that has to do with the blueprints."

"Didn't Collin mention that the iguanas are considered an endangered species on the island? Or something along those lines." When Joe agreed, I continued. "So even if Greenfield bought out the land on Turtle Cove, they likely couldn't build there unless they got permission from the island. I don't know how that would work, but it sounds expensive."

"I can reach out to my friend back in King City that deals with real estate law. He'll probably know best."

"That's great," I said. "But it still wouldn't explain why Robert was hiding the prints and what they have to do with Greenfield Industries."

Joe scratched his chin. "Well, he was an architect

for the company. It would make sense he'd have all the plans and blueprints for every project."

"Yes, but why go to the trouble of hiding them? And why these plans specifically?" I glanced at the laptop again. "There's a story here. I can feel it."

Taking the phone from me, Joe closed the laptop and reached for my hand. I took it and he pulled me up, his arm around my waist. In the distance, the sound of seagulls fighting over food scraps drifted down the beach, their loud squawking the only interruption to the surrounding solitude.

I looked up at Joe through my lashes. "What are you thinking?"

"There's a cozy little place called Le Petit Elephant on the other side of the island. Let's get out of here and go check it out," he suggested. "Supposedly, they have the best coffee you'll ever taste."

"You had me at coffee," I told Joe. Gesturing to the laptop, I asked, "But what about all this? We're on the brink of getting somewhere, I'm certain of it."

Joe wiggled his bushy brows. "Don't worry, the trip is both business and pleasure."

He pulled me in closer and turned us around so we faced the villa. With another pull, he walked us through the sliding doors and toward the front entrance. My eyes narrowed as he opened the door and handed me my purse.

"What are you scheming?" I asked.

"Nothing at all," Joe said.

I pouted, my lips forming a slight downturn as scepticism colored my expression. "Why the sudden interest in the French place? It can't be only for a good cup of coffee, which I obviously would never say no to. You're up to something."

"Trust me, this outing will be worth your time," Joe reassured me, his tone holding a hint of mystery.

"Because of a latte?" I asked incredulously, raising an eyebrow in disbelief.

Joe's gaze softened as he reached for my hand, determined. He planted a soft kiss on it before closing the door behind us and securing it with a definitive click. "Because according to Fallon's social media, Les Petit Elephant is his favorite spot on the island," he explained, his voice low with a hint of excitement. Diving into the pocket of his shorts, he retrieved his phone and pulled up Fallon's profile, displaying a series of images capturing the man's trademark grin against the backdrop of the charming restaurant. Joe enlarged the photo, emphasizing his point. "And he just so happens to be there right now. If we hurry, we can catch him before he leaves."

A surge of curiosity mingled with anticipation coursed through me, adding an extra layer of intrigue to our impromptu excursion. I was even more in the mood for French coffee now.

CHAPTER
14

The first thing I realized when we reached the French restaurant was that Joe was an expert driver. The streets of the neighborhood the restaurant was located in were so narrow, one had to basically scale the walls to get through without running into oncoming traffic. By some miracle, we found a parking spot in a lot smaller than my closet back home and Joe crammed the car in between two large pickup trucks. As we walked from the lot to Le Petit Elephant, I made a note of small shops selling handmade jewelry I wanted to stop in at after we were done.

As the street narrowed further, I found myself navigating past a lumbering van emerging from the opposite side. Amidst the bustle, my gaze wandered to the right, where Le Petit Elephant stood like an oasis amidst the chaos. The quaintness of the scene was almost palpable, as if plucked from a storybook.

The restaurant's front patio, a cozy enclave barely spacious enough for two petite round tables, was held up by sturdy columns, one of which proudly displayed an intricately designed menu. Beyond the threshold, the shuttered doors beckoned invitingly, their opening a welcome for all.

Taking a moment to absorb the scene, I couldn't help but grin at the sight that greeted me. The walls, painted in a soft, muted yellow hue, served as a canvas for exquisite Renaissance artwork. Cherubs frolicked amidst idyllic landscapes, while scenes of sun-drenched picnics exuded an air of timeless leisure.

My eyes wandered to the left, drawn to a patisserie-style display brimming with an array of delectable treats, each one a scrumptious temptation. Behind this culinary spectacle, another room lay concealed behind yet another shuttered door— undoubtedly the heart of the establishment, the kitchen.

My eyes spotted a glass cellar with rows of delectable wine, and I nudged Joe with my elbow. "This place is adorable."

"Agreed," he said. He scanned the seating area, his

chin tipping lightly in the direction of a middle-aged man dressed in an expensive, well-tailored suit. "That's our guy."

I watched from the patio as Fallon Boatman perused the menu in front of him. His gelled hair was slicked back and stood so high up off his head that it appeared to be levitating. If I didn't know better, I'd guess he was a warlock and magic was involved. Just to be sure, I checked for a talisman, but found none.

The developer looked at the screen of his phone and his eyes rolled skyward. He typed out a quick message and let out a frustrated sigh, then proceeded to rattle off his order to the server who was waiting patiently at the table.

My eyes flicked to Joe. "A real winner, huh?"

"Let's get a table and get this over with."

After requesting a seat toward the rear, strategically positioned next to Fallon, we were graciously escorted to our table, where menus awaited us. Each page made me smack my lips in delight, detailing specials crafted to tempt. Despite having indulged in a meal merely an hour ago, my mouth watered uncontrollably as I scanned the list. Deciding to treat myself, I settled on an appetizer of escargot, served in a rich garlic butter sauce, accompanied by a macchiato presented in a martini glass, its aroma invading my nose. Meanwhile, Joe, ever the gentleman, chose the

Provencal Onion Tart, its delicate layers of pastry and caramelized onions a sight to be seen. With a subtle nudge, he slide the dish toward me after I finished my own meal. It was moments like these that reminded me why Joe was not merely a perfect man, but indeed an angel in vampire form.

Having spent a decent enough time pretending to be natural, Joe winked and turned to Fallon's table.

"Fallon?" he asked. "Fallon Boatman?"

Annoyance flashed over the developer's face as he looked up from his cellphone to face Joe. His demeanor quickly switched when he noticed my boyfriend and I wondered if it was because of Joe's generally welcoming appearance. Whatever the reason, his shoulders relaxed, and he put the phone away to give Joe his full attention.

"One and the same," he said.

"What a small world," Joe exclaimed, turning his chair to inch closer to the man. "I'm Joe and this is Piper. We're good friends with one of your guys at Greenfield."

Fallon arched one manicured brow. "Oh, yeah? Which one?"

"Old Bobby Atlas."

Bobby? Wow. I had to hand it to Joe. He was really selling our cover. It seemed I had not given my guy enough credit; he was great at playing a part. Guilt clawed its way up my chest. I pushed it down, vowing to never leave Joe out of my sneaky plans again. Especially since he made for such a wonderful wing man.

Across from us, Fallon's eyes darkened and his hand reached for his phone again. I cleared my throat, dragging his attention from Joe to me. "We're very sorry for your loss," I said quickly.

"Oh. Thank you. Piper, is it?"

I nodded, twisting around in the chair to get a better view of the man. The self-assured expression he had on a second ago was gone and in its place was something I couldn't quite put my finger on. If I had to guess, I'd say Fallon was not pleased to be running into the dead man's supposed friends.

Ignoring the warning bells in my head, I took a sip of my macchiato and sat the glass down. The coffee sloshed around and dripped down the sides. "It must be hard to lose someone you knew so well," I pressed on.

"We weren't all that close."

"Oh?" I scratched my head. "I thought your wives were friends."

I must have caught him off guard, because Fallon's stoic expression faltered and his otherwise blank eyes sparked. He looked between me and Joe, his hands fisting. "As much as I feel for Carla during this time, I'm sorry to say that I never liked the woman. I told my wife as much, but she refused to agree. Spent way too much time with those two, if you ask me."

"Really? Carla seemed very genuine to me," Joe said.

"She wasn't," Fallon corrected. He reached for a glass of water and downed it in one go. "That woman had poor Robert wrapped around her finger. I tried to warn him, but he wouldn't listen. Not sure what he saw in her, but I guess my wife saw the same thing. Carla had that effect on people."

The way he emphasized the word made the hairs on the back of my neck stand on edge. I kept my back rigid and tried not to make eye contact with Joe, whose gaze I could feel burn into the side of my face. Fallon's words repeated in my head. Was he implying she was cheating on Robert?

Only one way to find out.

I sucked in a breath and let it go slowly. "Did you think Carla may have reciprocated someone's interest?"

"I don't think it," Fallon said with a scoff. "I know it."

"Who?"

He shook his head. "Too many to list, I'd imagine. The one that comes to mind is that landlord of theirs. Collin something or other. It was so obvious the way they flirted right in front of Robert." He readjusted his tie and checked the designer watch on his wrist. "That's why I didn't want Monica spending time with the woman. In case she started getting any ideas."

I watched Fallon's hands, still in tight fists, and my stomach turned. Did he use those fists often? The way Monica spoke about him gave me the impression that she was afraid of her husband, and now that I met Fallon in person, I could see why. He had all the markings of a control freak down pat.

Swallowing my anger, I shifted in the chair, my entire body straight as an arrow.

"How did you two know Robert, by the way?"

I gulped.

Beside me, Joe was quicker and thought on his feet. His lips curled, and he flashed Fallon his pearly whites. Relief washed over me when I didn't see his fangs pop out. "We were looking to invest in some property on the island," Joe lied. "It's why we're here, actually. Robert mentioned your company is working on a big development."

"Yes, of course! The resort on Runaway Coast."

"Hmm," Joe mused. "I thought he said it was on an isle somewhere. Turtle Cove, if I recall correctly."

The color drained from Fallon's face, and his eyes darted around the room like a deer caught in headlights. He swallowed hard, his Adam's apple bobbing up and down with so much force I thought it would jump into his mouth. Palm flattening on the table, his gaze flickered as it landed on Joe. "You must be mistaken," he said. "We don't own land there. But we did recently acquire a great spot on St. Howard. If you're serious about getting in on the ground floor, I can take you over later next week. I was there for the last month, setting the site up and it is a beauty."

"Perhaps," Joe said. "How far off is it from us?"

"About an hour's flight," Fallon answered. "I only got back last night myself, but I'll be making another trip over." He reached into his jacket and pulled out a shiny black business card, handing it to Joe. "Give me a call and I can meet you there."

Rising to stand, Fallon motioned for the server to bring a check and the young man hurried to deliver. Paying, Fallon checked his watch again, saying, "I must get back to the office. It was great meeting you two."

"Same here," Joe said, while I forced a sad smile. "And thanks for the invitation."

Fallon's face brightened for the first time since we got here. "No problem," he said, walking out. "Anything for Robert's friends."

As I watched his back retreat, butterflies swirled in my belly. Fallon Boatman was lying. I didn't know what about, but I was certain he was hiding something. Could he be the one who had killed Robert? I didn't think he'd get his hands dirty, but Fallon could definitely afford to hire a hit man. Yet why?

If anything, it was clear he hated Carla and not Robert. Then there was the accusation he threw around so carelessly about her. The more I got to know of the Atlases, the more confused I became. This seemingly normal couple was anything but. Between the fight we witnessed, Robert's strange murder, and all the rumors surrounding the two, I was beginning to suspect that the Atlases harbored secrets so deep, they may never be uncovered.

I reached for Joe's hand. "Fancy a swim before the sun goes down?"

"What about your investigation?"

My chest rose and fell with deep, even breaths. "Forget it," I told him. "I think it's time we do what we came here for and relax. No more sleuthing. No more murder talk. From now on, it's only us and the beach."

CHAPTER 15

I could not forget it at all. The mere thought that our landlord could somehow be involved in a murder was driving me up the wall. Literally. I balanced on one foot as I stretched higher to reach the top shelf. My fingers grazed the handle of the cup and I yanked it down, losing my balance on the chair I teetered on. My falling body picked up speed. I yelped, eyes shutting as I prepared to hit the ground.

Two strong arms swept under me as Joe used his vampire speed to zoom from the living room to the kitchen. He set me down gently, taking the cup from my trembling hands.

"I could have gotten that down for you," he said.

I brushed down the folds of my mid-length dress,

taking the cup back. "I know. But I have to do something with myself or I'll crawl out of my skin."

"Can't relax, can you?"

Wincing, I set the cup on the bar table and proceeded to pour the frothy coffee mixture I blended into it. I added a dollop of freshly whipped cream and sprinkled some cinnamon on top. Lips curling around a straw, I took a sip so long I got a brain freeze. "Maybe I'm not cut out for vacations."

"Challenge accepted," Joe said with a chuckle. "I'm making it my life's mission to take you on at least one getaway without a dead body."

A laugh burst out of me and some of the coffee came out of my nose. I laughed harder, Joe joining in. Putting the cup down, I wiped the tears in my eyes and said, "I'm afraid you'll fail. Don't forget you're talking to the daughter of Hades here."

Sliding across the island, Joe wrapped an arm around me and I melted into his strong chest. Despite all the ways I messed up while we were here, he was still there for me, still the rock I needed to get through things. Now that I mentioned my father, a chill filled the air and my head spun. Mom was due for a call today and I worried she wouldn't have good news to deliver. With everything that had gone down next door, I had completely forgotten about the Sisters of the River and the threat they posed to the world. Stella would say that was the entire point of the vacation, but I begged to differ. I couldn't let my guard down, not until I knew what to expect from Hades.

It's possible we were all wrong and he could be reasoned with.

I shook my head, pressing my cheek deeper into Joe's chest. Only I would be foolish enough to try to reason with the devil.

"Being related to him does not make you like him," Joe said.

I bristled. "Do you think there's a chance he's not as bad as Mom makes him out to be?" I asked with a sigh. "She made it seem that the Sisters were the worst out there, but when I met Linna Cruller, she was pretty normal. Mom might be wrong about Hades too."

"Anything is possible. Sylvie does strike me as being a bit dramatic."

A chuckle escaped me. *You have no idea.*

While I cleaned up the kitchen, Joe went upstairs to get our beach towels and met me at the back doors. We decided to make it our mission to spend as much time in the water as we could before our flight home, and so far, we'd been making good on that promise. Sure, there had been a few hiccups along the way on account of Robert's death and my inability to leave things alone, but we were back on track now.

As I waded into the bathlike water, I felt my entire body relax. Every muscle moved with the tide and I sank deeper and deeper into the crystal clear ocean. My toes grazed the sand, and I flipped backward, floating like I used to do when I was a kid and Mom would take me to the local pool. Above me, the sun streamed its welcoming beams and my face warmed as its fingers caressed my skin.

This was what heaven must be.

A splash of water covered me and I sputtered, flipping back around to stand. My eyes blinked away the salty water. I whipped around, seeing Joe readying to splash me again. I growled playfully. "You're going down, vampire!"

"Bring it, witch!"

My hands tingled, the magic inside me getting riled up. One good thing about Joe was I didn't have to hide being a paranormal near him and though we were definitely not a regular couple—witches and vampires didn't exactly co-mingle—at least we were matched in power. Where Joe was super strong and fast, I had my own brand of oddball magic thanks to Father dearest. Grinning mischievously, I pushed my palms under the water and waited for the energy in my fingers to build. When it felt like I might explode, I let the magic the loose.

The surrounding water swooshed and bubbled as I

used my power to raise it high in the air. I wasn't sure what I was doing but since Hades had control of the Underworld and the river flowing through it, I figured I may have inherited the gene. It appeared I did. Water skyrocketed around me and I couldn't see Joe's face anymore, though I knew he was impressed. When it was too high to hold, I slammed my hands back to the surface, and the water crashed back into the ocean.

I heard Joe let out a yelp and duck under as the last of it came down. A moment later, he emerged, his hair soaked and his eyes blinking away my epic splash.

He ran a hand down his face. "Well played."

"I learned a new trick," I said, beaming.

"I see that."

As Joe treaded toward me, a flash of movement on the beach caught my eye. I turned away from him to see what it was, but the sand was abandoned. Craning my neck, I surveyed up and down the beach and couldn't see anyone at all.

"What is it?" Joe asked.

My eyes checked the beach one last time. "Thought I saw something. You think Carla is back?"

"I doubt it," Joe said. "Unfortunately, I fear she may have met the same tragic end as her husband. Could be Collin."

"Possibly."

The mention of the landlord put him right back in

the forefront of my mind. I was trying so hard not to get involved. Tough to do considering that we were not only staying next door to the victim but shared his landlord. Especially since I now had reason to believe that the same landlord wasn't as innocent as he made himself out to be.

Could Collin have made up the lie about Monica and Robert to throw me off his trail? If he thought we were digging around where we shouldn't have been, he may have lied to buy himself time. But to do what, exactly? As tempting as it was, I didn't want to jump to conclusions.

The landlord had a connection to Robert, was known to have harassed him over the rent, and was possibly having relations with his wife. It was as though every finger pointed at Collin. While I didn't want to admit it, it was very possible that the killer was under our noses the entire time.

A light wave knocked me off my feet and Joe caught me before I face planted into the ocean. "Let me guess," he said. "We're not quite finished with the Atlas case."

I winced.

"All right, spill it. What's the plan?"

Wading in the water, I swayed from side to side with the tide. The warmth of the ocean cocooned me and in another universe, one where I wasn't so obsessed with solving crimes, I could stay in this moment forever. Unfortunately for me, and for Joe, I was a dog with a bone now. I pushed my palm out, playfully splashing Joe again. "I want to talk to Collin again."

"Finally," Joe breathed out. "I was wondering when you were going to come out and say it."

"You knew I'd cave so fast?"

He laughed under his breath. "In your defense, you held out way longer than I thought."

"So you're all right with doing more snooping?"

As Joe took my hand, I knew the answer. "Already accepted it as part of the deal with dating you," he said, kissing my forehead. "And I texted Collin this morning to meet us next door later."

I wrapped my arms around Joe's thick next and pulled him in. The water made me so light, I drifted around him like a sheet of silk. Ocean waves shifted us in the sand, but Joe's strong stance held on, solid and dependable. "You're the best, you know that?" I said, swooning.

"You won't think that after this."

"After what?" I asked.

I was too late. Joe was already lifting me high over his head to throw me into the water. His laughter boomed around us as I flew and when I hit the water again, I let it swallow me whole. A peace unlike any other overcoming me.

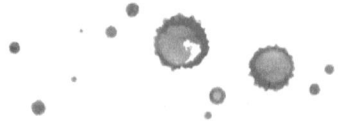

We spent the rest of the afternoon swimming and sunbathing. By the time we dragged our exhausted bodies back into the villa, I could barely make it up the stairs. Which isn't surprising since those things were tough to climb on a good day. I let Joe take a go at the shower first and settled in on the window seat in the bedroom to check my phone.

Things back home were fine. Or sort of kind of fine, as Cilia put it. Apparently, Rory had taken it upon herself to turn the office into her own magic sanctuary and remodeled it to be a fortress. When I asked how Harry was going to be able to come in and out, I was guaranteed that the young witch had it handled. Any other business owner would have been upset, but not me. I was relieved that Rory wasn't practicing her skills by adding items on the menu since the last time we ended up with a coffee disaster on our hands.

Besides, the girl could use to work more on her craft. Me, too, now that I thought about it.

A new text popped up as I typed a reply to my friend and I quickly switched conversation threads when I saw my mom's name. My eyes narrowed on her long text chain, heart racing with every word. I stretched my legs, then pulled them back into my chest again, my fingers white-knuckling the phone case. So much information to receive in such a short amount of time. I was about to dial Mom's number, but stopped. There was no knowing who was around and if a Sister saw my name, it might blow Mom's cover.

With trepidation, I put the phone down on the bench beside me and stared at it like it was a bomb.

"Bad news?"

I twisted to Joe standing in the doorway, fresh out of the shower. He ran a towel over his wet hair, his green eyes studying me at the window. "No, not bad," I replied. "Mom finally messaged."

"What did the spy have to say?"

"Looks like Isabella's information panned out, and she has the location for the blood moon ritual next month. She said she has a plan to sabotage the Sisters' spell before the big date, but she needs me to do it. And you apparently. I have no idea why."

Joe tossed the towel into the dirty laundry bin in the corner of the room. "Hey, if it stops Hades from crossing over into our realm, I'm happy to help."

"Right, yeah."

Why do I not sound happy? Am I happy? It was becoming increasingly difficult to gauge my feelings about my father's plan to leave the Underworld. Rationally, I knew nothing good could come out of this and yet... Yet I was still the same little girl who didn't know where she came from and would do anything to meet her dad.

Talk about daddy issues.

I rubbed my temples, the pressure building there subsiding briefly, and focused on Joe. "Ready to go next door? I'll shower when we're back before dinner."

Nodding, Joe threw on a short-sleeve button-down shirt the color of the sky and waited while I laced up my sandals. I took his hand, walking down the stairs carefully, so I didn't break my neck before we had a chance to confront Collin. As we crossed the backyard and slipped around the side to the Atlas's property, my stomach sank. The house was dark, not a light on. At our back, the setting sun painted the villa in a shade of deep pink and cast ominous shadows from our bodies onto the stucco. I recoiled at the shadow of a growing figure in a pointy hat on the wall. Turning around with the speed of light, I breathed out a relieved breath when I realized it came from a gnome statue nestled in the backyard. Twisting back, I followed Joe to inch closer. From here, Joe and I looked like nightmare monsters approaching, our pitch-black versions stretching like gnarled fingers.

I glanced behind me, hoping Stella was around, but she was yet to return from her escapades on the island. No matter, I had Joe. Then what was that dread settling deep in my chest? "Something feels off," I murmured, my grip tightening on Joe's reassuring hand. "I don't like this."

He tipped his chin in the direction of the open back door. "Me neither. I like that even less."

"Do you think Collin is in there?" A thought popped into my head. "Perhaps whoever was here last time turning the place upside down is back. We should call the police."

"Agreed," Joe said. "You do that and I'll go see if I can find Collin."

He left me in the backyard and slid into the darkness of the villa, his back retreating until I couldn't see him at all. Following the plan, I dialed the number Detective Sanders left us and waited. After a few rings, his voicemail greeted me on the other end. I left a quick, convoluted message that I hoped he would understand and took a few steps closer to the door. "Joe?"

There was no answer.

My legs trembled, the weight of my body suddenly too much for them to handle. Joe could handle himself. He was a big, bad vampire. Right? I couldn't take the risk. One foot over the threshold and the other hovering outside, I tried him again. "Joe? Are you there?"

After a few minutes, I heard a distant curse.

"Joe?"

"I'm here!" he yelled out from the darkness. "Did you call the police?"

My brow furrowed. "I did. What's going on? Did you find Collin?"

When Joe didn't answer, I took the leap and rushed inside. As I darted through the house, I heard Joe shout for me to stay out, but it was too late. I was already at the bottom of the stairs by the time I realized what he was saying. I was already staring at Joe crouching on the floor, his massiveness obscuring what lay there. My lips were already trembling at the sight of two legs bent at odd angles sticking out from behind my boyfriend.

A shiver tripped down my spine. "Is that...Collin?"

"Afraid so," Joe said solemnly.

"Is he...?"

Joe didn't have to answer. His eyes said it all. Chest heaving, I stepped around him and dared to look down. It was dark but my eyes had adjusted to the light by now, unfortunately. Perhaps if I were still blind, I wouldn't have had to see Collin's lifeless gaze landing past my right ankle. I crunched my teeth together, buckling back a few steps.

"Good thing you called the police," Joe said.

I didn't answer. There was nothing good about any of this.

CHAPTER 16

We stood awkwardly by the tall fence separating our property from the villa next door. My shoulder rubbed against a palm tree, the rough surface scratching my skin and bringing me back to reality. After we found Collin and the police arrived, Joe insisted on searching for new accommodations but I asked him to stay. At least for the time being. The idea of packing and moving in the midst of all this was too much to handle.

Then there was the matter of settling with...well, I didn't know whom anymore. With Collin dead, whom did we contact about the rental, anyway?

Detective Sanders waved to someone inside the villa through the glass doors. "You mentioned seeing someone while you were on the beach," he said. "Can you recall approximately what time that was?"

I scratched my head, unsure.

"Around two in the afternoon," Joe answered. "I can't be one hundred percent certain, but that seems about right. Doesn't it, Piper?"

I nodded. My throat felt a few sizes too small and my chest ached as though someone were sitting on it. Being a magnet for death was not the greatest for vacationing. I rubbed my gums with my tongue. "Have you found Carla yet?"

"We have people scouring the island and several search parties have been formed," the detective answered. "No luck yet."

My face blanched as Joe squeezed my hand, dangling at my side. I had the distinct feeling that we were thinking the same thing—Carla would not be found. At least not alive.

Flashes of Monica's sour expression drifted by me and I froze. Another wife caught in a possibly dangerous marriage. Fallon was quick to point the finger at Collin and for him to turn up conveniently dead was too much of a coincidence. I didn't trust the developer. What was it that Gran always said? Where there was money, there was trouble, and Fallon Boatman had a ton of it.

"Have you looked into Greenfield Industries?" I asked the detective.

His features shifted, mouth forming a large O. I'd caught him by surprise with the question. Either the police hadn't thought to look into Robert's employer or they did and didn't find anything. I wondered which one it was going to be. When Harding spoke, I had my answer.

"I'm not sure I follow," Sanders said. "What would Greenfield Industries have to do with what happened here today?"

My body froze. "Wait, you don't think the two deaths are related?"

"I don't know what theories you have been speculating on," the detective said with a scoff, "but what happened to your landlord was an accident. I must admit the timing isn't great, but there was evidence of him doing work on the villa in the upstairs hallway. He must have slipped and fell down the stairs, at least that is what we can gather based on the trajectory of his fall and where the body ended up. There is nothing to suggest foul play so you can rest at ease. Be careful on those stairs, though. Don't know who thought they were a good idea, but clearly, they are not safe at all."

As he glanced inside the villa to check on the team working there, I shared twin looks of worry with Joe.

The police were not even remotely close to finding out who killed Robert, not if what the detective said was true. How could they not see the two deaths were obviously related? My jaw clicked. Probably because they never bothered to talk to Fallon. Though I had the notion that even if they did, nothing would come out of it. If my experience back home taught me anything, it was that the cops followed evidence, which was fine and dandy until there was none.

My gut told me differently and I had learned enough to follow its direction.

Out of the corner of my eye, I saw a white sheet being lowered to cover Collin's body and my fingers tingled. The anxiety tripped up my magic and I could already feel it claw its way to the surface. I looked down at my fingers to check if they were acting up and shoved them in the pockets of my long dress, just in case. Beside me, Joe noticed and lifted his brows.

"We'll take it easy on the stairs," he said. "Are we free to go, or do you have any more questions?"

The detective shook his head and let us know he'd be in touch if he needed us again. I was getting tired of being on this guy's call list. No matter what trouble I may have had with Sheriff Romero, I never questioned his ability to do his job. Sanders, on the other hand, appeared to be as competent with law enforcement as I was with makeup application. Or he didn't care enough to put his all into this investigation. There was also the possibility that he wasn't telling us everything because we were suspects, but I tried not to dwell on that option.

Following Joe back to our villa, I kept my eyes on the ground and my lips shut until we were out of earshot of Sanders and the police. "They're way off base," I whispered when we were in the clear.

"Sadly, very much so," Joe agreed. "It's odd they wouldn't follow up on Greenfield or Collin's death more."

I reached for a chiffon scarf I'd left on the backrest of the seat outside and wrapped it around my shoulders. "Should we tell them about the blueprints and what Fallon said about Collin and Carla?"

"I wouldn't," Joe answered, surprising me. "It doesn't appear that they care enough, and if your hunch is correct and Greenfield is to blame for all of this, they might muck it up even more. But we should sleep on it and see how we feel in the morning. To be honest, I'm starting to wonder if we're grasping at straws ourselves here."

"I know what you mean. It's as though there's one big piece missing and it's the one that makes the entire puzzle come together."

A low laugh filled the backyard, drifting over the sound of the crashing waves not far from us. I looked at Joe, his eyes twinkling in the moonlight and the glow of the two lamps on either side of us. "What's so funny?"

"Nothing," he said, still chuckling. "You're very determined, that's all."

"It would be lovely if you could be as determined by your fashion choices. I mean really, Piper. Chiffon?"

My heart jumped into my throat at Stella's voice. I twisted around, gaze rolling down the ghost's body as she hovered on the pathway between us and the beach. "Stella! Finally. Where have you been?"

"Hi, Stella," Joe echoed from behind me.

The ghost waved a bored hand as though the motion explained her absence. "I may be your familiar, Piper, but you are not my keeper," she said. "This is my vacation too, you know."

"Sure," I gritted out. "A little warning next time. There is a killer on the loose?"

Stella quirked one perfectly manicured brow. "Really? Kind of already dead if you haven't noticed."

"Good point. So, did you see anything worth mentioning?"

Another hand wave and an eyeroll were all I got from the ghost. Instead of answering, she pointed to the small collection of rocks separating the path she stood on from an identical one beside it leading to the

Atlas villa. "I see something over there you might want to check out."

Glancing at Joe, I called him over to follow me and walked toward Stella. My eyes tracked the direction she pointed all the way to a small gap between the rocks. Inside, something small glinted as the moonlight hit it. A small object that anyone was sure to miss unless they were looking.

I crouched down and dug my fingers in between the rocks to pull it out. As I did, I held it up to Joe and Stella, twisting it around. "What's an earring doing over there?"

"A diamond earring at that," Stella added. "An expensive one, too. I'd say that sucker is at least two carats."

"How do you know it's real?"

The ghost scoffed. "Please, Piper. If there is one thing I know, it's diamonds. And that one is as real as they come. You should see if you can pawn it, I bet it's worth a fortune. Or better yet, turn it into a pendant and finally get rid of that gaudy necklace you always wear."

My hand instinctively reached for the wishbone pendant on my collar. "This was Gran's," I told the ghost.

The light hit the earrings in my grip once more and the bright sparkle of the diamond drew me in. I brought it closer, inspecting the piece from every angle. I'd seen this earring before.

I jumped up and ran into the house, returning with my phone. Scrolling through the gallery, I pulled up the photo I snapped when we first discovered Robert's body. The one of the Atlases together. Zooming in on Carla, I gasped, then turned the screen around so Joe and Stella could see it too. "That's Carla's earring. I'm certain of it."

"Why would it be wedged all the way there?" Joe asked. "You'd think she'd notice she's missing that big rock."

I trailed the path to the villa next door. The lights were on but the police seemed to be wrapping up with what happened earlier because there were only a few officers left behind and they were all gathered near the front. My eyes scanned the villa, jaw working as I thought.

"We should give them the earring," Joe said, pointing to the officers. "It might be important evidence that could help them find Carla."

I barely heard him, my mind racing. "What if Carla saw what happened to Robert, and the killer got to her, too? The earring could have been knocked out of her ear during a struggle."

"Wouldn't there be more evidence of that?" Stella asked.

I scratched the back of my head. "Unless they snatched her here and took her somewhere else," I mused. "Could it be Collin figured out who did it and was going to tell us, but they got to him first?"

"Why us, though?" Joe asked. "Why not go straight to the police?"

"I don't know. But if he had the same feelings about the police as we do, I doubt he'd trust them with the truth. And you did tell him I was some sort of genius when it came to solving crimes."

"I believe he said savant," Stella corrected. "Don't build yourself up, it's uncouth."

My shoulders drooped. "How did you know what Joe said? Never mind, explain later. You two know what this means, don't you?"

Next to me, Joe said something about canceling our dinner reservations for tomorrow, and Stella complained about my inability to relax. I blocked them both out, concentrating instead on the threads hanging before me. The jumble of possible clues was slowly starting to come together. I could nearly pull out a concrete theory to clarify the chaos. Somehow, and I didn't know how yet, Fallon Boatman was in the middle of it all. I needed to listen to Gran. I had to follow the money.

Checking on the police again, I shook my head in disappointment. If they weren't going to check every angle, I would. Carla was still out there somewhere. I wanted to find her, dead or alive. It was as though I was drawn to solving this mystery by some invisible force, and it was stronger than any rational part of me. I grimaced.

I think it's time to admit that this is no longer a vacation. We have a killer to catch and a woman to find. I looked up at the moon, breathing in deeply. *And less than three days left to do it.*

Joe Brooks

Watching Piper pretend to relax was like walking into a haunted house at a carnival; you knew someone was going to jump out of the shadows, but you still jumped each time. I felt the same way as I studied her face and waited for her to finally say what she was thinking. There was a chance she wouldn't share it again and run off on her own, heading nose first into trouble. I hoped I'd convinced her that it wasn't necessary this time. That I didn't need her to act any certain way and that who she was at her core was enough.

More than enough, really.

One of the best things about Piper Addison was her insistence on getting to the truth no matter what. Did I wish that the woman I fell for didn't have a need to solve every murder she stumbled into? Sure. But did I also admire her for wanting justice for victims who couldn't speak for themselves? Definitely.

And as Piper said, death was quite literally in her blood, so I had to respect that.

I poured another glass of iced coffee into her cup and left her to chat with Stella on the beach. While the women talked, I took the chance to remove one of the conveniently packed vegan blood bags I'd purchased from a paranormal shop earlier this week from the fridge and placed it on the counter. The smell of plastic and iron filled my nostrils as I poured out the contents into a tall glass. When I first decided to opt for lab-created blood instead of its human counterpart, I thought it would be hard to manage. Being a vampire had its bonuses, but the blood craving was everything the stories told you. Without it, I would perish. Worse, I would first go completely insane then I would perish.

It was the main reason most vampires still drank human blood.

I shivered. The mere thought of it repulsed me now. It had been years since I'd had it and I was glad for it. My family, on the other hand...well, that was a different story. Those monsters were best left in the past.

Downing the reddish tinged drink, I rinsed off the glass and placed it in the dishwasher. From here, I had a clear view of Piper's animated gestures as she explained something to Stella, who no doubt had a lot to say back. The ghost was hilarious and I couldn't even see or hear her.

The perfect familiar for my girl.

Outside, Piper pulled on her ear as she spoke. I knew what she was thinking, instantly. The earring she found last night was weighing heavily on her and much as she tried, I could tell she was itching to follow up on the clue. I couldn't blame her. I was quite interested myself.

Shutting the dishwasher, I grabbed my phone from the island and dialed a number I knew by heart. The line rang several times, then a low, grumbly voice sounded on the other end.

"You better be calling about a lead on the coven," Brian said.

Brian, my paranormal private detective and college buddy, was always on me about the vampire coven he'd been trying to hunt down for ages. My parents' vampire coven, to be exact. One thing I was yet to tell Piper was about the sordid past with my family and that their coven was the main reason why.

How did you tell a woman you were in love with that you were the son of two of the most brutal vampires to ever exist?

It wasn't only the fear of her rejection that held me back; it was the weight of the legacy I carried, a legacy steeped in darkness and bloodshed. My parents, revered and feared among vampires, were responsible for countless atrocities, their names whispered in hushed tones even among our kind. The thought of revealing this truth to Piper filled me with dread.

I mean, seriously, there would be books written about the atrocities my family had committed if anyone could find them. The history of my lineage was woven with the screams of victims and the stains of innocent blood. It was a burden I bore silently, a burden that threatened to consume me if I dared to confront it.

I never wanted anything to do with their horrific ways of existing, which was why I split the second I could get away. Hadn't talked to anyone in the family since. Fleeing from that suffocating environment was my only chance at redemption, my only hope of forging a different path. But no matter how far I ran, their shadows loomed over me, a constant reminder of who I was and where I came from. And now, as I grappled with the prospect of revealing the truth to Piper, those shadows seemed darker and more menacing than ever before.

Come to think of it, the only time I ever thought of them was when Brian brought them up. Which was often since he had it in his brain that he was going to find them and bring them to justice. A tough task, even for an alpha of a werewolf pack.

I scowled, turning on the wash cycle. "Nothing since we talked last," I told him. "How's the pack? Lisa and the girls doing well?"

"Growing like weeds. Maylene had her first shift last week."

I let out a low whistle. "Girl wolf," I said. "Congrats, man."

"Thanks," Brian answered. The pride in his voice was unmistakable. "So why the call?"

"I was hoping you can run down a name for me. Get a contact number."

There was a long silence on the line and for a second I thought I had lost him. Finally, Brian huffed out an exhausted breath and asked, "What's the name?"

"Monica Boatman."

I heard the sound of pen on paper as Brian took down the name. "Do I even want to know what you need a woman's number for?"

"It's not what you think," I said with a chuckle.

"I'll explain when I see you next time, but trust me, this is for a good cause."

"Always is with you, Brooks," the wolf said.

Promising to get me something within the hour, he hung up, and I returned to watching Piper from the kitchen. She stretched her long legs on the sand, her toes buried and her back arched as she basked in the sunshine. Once I got her Monica's number, she'd be ready to go and excited to move forward with getting answers. I knew her enough to know that. Part of me hoped Brian wouldn't find anything so we could enjoy the rest of the trip, but there was no real chance of that. The wolf was the best in the business.

I glanced out the glass doors and smiled. Soon, we would be chasing down Monica and playing detective, possibly putting ourselves in mortal danger. But not yet. For now, until I had something from Brian, this was still a plain old boring vacation.

I snatched a bottle of sunscreen off the counter and squirted half a bottle's worth in my hands.

Let's make the best of it, witch, I thought as I slid open the doors and walked to the beach.

CHAPTER 18

The night wrapped itself around me like a shroud. I was tumbling down into a dark, endless abyss. I fell, my screams swallowed by the void, until I landed with a jolt on cold, damp earth.

Blinking away the disorientation, I stood up in a desolate landscape. The air was thick with an otherworldly chill, and shadows danced eerily around me. Before me stood the imposing gates of the Underworld, wrought from iron and adorned with grotesque carvings.

A chill ran down my spine as the gates creaked open, revealing a cavernous darkness within. Hesitantly, I stepped forward, my heart pounding in her chest. As I entered, the gates slammed shut behind me, sealing my fate within the realm of the dead.

"Welcome, daughter of mine," a deep, echoing voice reverberated through the darkness. My blood ran cold as I turned to face the source of the voice. Before me stood a figure cloaked in darkness, his eyes burning like smoldering embers in the gloom.

"Hades," I whispered, my voice trembling.

The god of the Underworld regarded me with a mixture of amusement and malice, his lips curling into a sinister smile.

My heart hammered in my chest as I glanced around, my surroundings shifting and warping with each passing moment. Ghostly apparitions floated by, their hollow eyes fixed on me with a chilling intensity.

"Please, I don't belong here," I stammered, my voice barely above a whisper.

But Hades only laughed.

"There is no escape from the Underworld," he said. "But perhaps, for the right price, I may grant you safe passage back to your world."

With a wave of his hand, Hades summoned a procession of ghosts, their wails filling the air with an otherworldly chorus. My eyes widened in terror as the ghosts closed in around me, their cold, clammy hands reaching out to grab me.

In a panic, I stumbled backward, body panicking

as I searched for a means of escape. But no matter which way I turned, I was surrounded by swirling darkness.

Just as all hope seemed lost, a voice cut through the chaos, echoing in my mind like a beacon of light.

"Piper, wake up!"

With a start, my eyes snapped open, my chest heaving as I gasped for breath. Blinking away the remnants of the nightmare, I found myself lying in bed, bathed in the soft glow of the sun outside the villa's bedroom window.

Relief flooded through me as I realized I was safe and sound. Not in the Underworld at all. Still here with Joe.

"Not the best nap, huh?" he asked.

I stared at the ceiling, shaking off the lingering remnants of fear. Shaking my head with a wry smile, I pushed it aside. Now was not the time to think about Hades or his nonsense. I turned in the bed, using my arm to rest on so I could look at Joe. "Nothing to worry about," I said. "Thanks for letting doze off for a bit."

"You looked like you needed it," he said, brushing the sweat-soaked hair from my brow. "And I have a surprise."

I shot up. "What kind of surprise?"

Joe laughed, dragging me back down. "The kind only you, Piper Addison, would like."

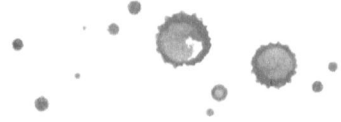

A hairbrush flew by my head, landing at my feet. I hopped over it, ignoring the rest of the mess on the floor of the bedroom as I got ready.

"You best not mess this up," Stella warned.

I rolled my eyes, pulling my shorts up. Looking in the mirror, I ran a finger over the fresh set of freckles dusting the bridge of my nose with a smile. The island sun was doing wonders for my complexion. Even with all the murders afoot.

Dusting a thin layer of blush on my cheeks, I rolled my hair into a top bun. "Is it your life's mission to annoy me?"

"Afterlife," Stella corrected. "And no. I am simply making sure that you appreciate what you have in front of you."

"I know how great Joe is," I told the ghost with a grunt.

A gray, sheer finger pointed in my face. I buckled back before Stella made contact with my skin and made both of us uncomfortable. The only thing worse than an ice-cold bath while listening to nails scratch a chalkboard was having a ghost touch you. Even after all the time I'd had to get used to it, shivers still tripped my spine each time it happened. Which was why Stella and I made a pact to avoid contact at all costs.

Unless one of us was upset with the other. Then all bets were off.

"Joe isn't great," Stella said, the finger still hovering. "A man who pulls your chair out at a restaurant is great. One that hunts down leads to help you solve a murder when you're on a vacation he paid for is on another level entirely."

My eyes rolled further.

"I'm serious, Piper," she scolded. "You're not getting any younger."

Blood boiling, I pushed my face into hers. "Move that finger or lose it."

Stella smirked, but floated a few feet back.

That's right.

Shoving past her, I risked the icky feeling and made sure my shoulder knocked through the ghost. Stella yelped in disgust and vanished, only to re-materialize outside in the hallway. Scowling, she followed me as I walked down the stairs to meet Joe. My fingers clung to the railing for dear life as flashes of Collin's dead body made unwelcome appearances before me. When I reached the bottom step, I nearly jumped for joy.

"Ready?" Joe asked.

I nodded, taking his outstretched hand.

"She still has to change," Stella said at my retreating back.

Glancing at her over my shoulder, I waved a fist. The ghost laughed. "Suit yourself," she said, before disappearing again. This time she stayed gone.

Grabbing my phone from the side table near the front entrance, I checked that I had everything I needed for the day before stepping outside with Joe. "Where are we meeting Monica again?" I asked as he unlocked the car.

"Runaway Cafe," Joe answered. "It's on the other side of the island. Should take us a half hour or so to get there."

I smiled, buckling in on the passenger side. "Thanks again for luring her out. Tell your friend I owe him big time for finding Monica's number. After I accosted her on Turtle Cove, I was pretty certain she'd never speak to me."

"It's no trouble at all. And she seemed eager to talk," Joe offered.

"Why did you think of her?"

Steering us out of the driveway, Joe sped down the road and onto the winding streets that cut through the island. He kept his eyes trained ahead when he said, "The way I see it, she's your best bet at getting any answers. She knew both victims and her husband sounds like a shady character. In my experience, when there's foul play of any kind, you follow the money. At least that's what I used to do with my clients."

"Did you work on murder cases when you were a lawyer?"

My stomach turned. The idea that Joe may have defended killers in his past didn't sit well with me. I knew that lawyers didn't always get to choose their clients, but it still made me feel all kinds of queasy inside.

"Not murder, no," Joe said. I let go of a breath I was holding. "But a lot of embezzlement charges. They're surprisingly similar in my opinion. People are willing to go far for the right price. It feels like that might be true in this case as well."

"You think Fallon Boatman is behind all this?"

Joe glanced in the rearview mirror, then took a left turn. "I think we're about to find out."

"If Monica tells us the truth."

"If she does," Joe agreed.

The car swerved along and I watched the ocean out of the window as we drove. Rays of glistening sun shimmered on the surface, the water so still today it looked like glass. I couldn't wait to go swimming later. I also couldn't wait to see what Monica had to offer and if Joe's suspicions about her husband were true.

We pulled around a corner and my breath hitched. The view of the island before us was something out of a travel brochure. The ocean went on forever and the palm-filled hills framed it in a picture-perfect arrangement on either side. Small stucco villas sat nestled in the hills, people living in their slices of heaven. The road turned down. I watched in awe as we neared a small marina. A large cruise ship was parked in the water—the first one I'd seen since the day we'd arrived on the island—and there were yachts and boats docked at designated spots.

"Nice place," Joe said as he parallel parked us behind a shiny black SUV.

I unbuckled my seatbelt and pressed my nose to the window. "Is that the cafe? It's adorable."

Runaway Cafe was a mix between the secret garden and a French bistro. White trellises with climbing ivy obscured the main building from view, the most luscious tropical flowers blooming around the property. There were two massive palm trees on either side of the entrance to a cobblestone path leading to the main cafe. Alongside it, round tables with freshly adorned flower vases lined the path, a small lantern beside each one. I could see a deck around the back with more tables and an uninterrupted view of the water.

"Just wow," I said as I climbed out of the car.

We walked hand in hand to the main entrance, finding it surprisingly locked. Joe and I exchanged twin looks of worry seconds before a frazzled employee stuck his head around the side of the building.

"Hi, folks," he said with a warm smile. "We're a little behind, if you don't mind waiting."

"No trouble at all," Joe said.

I rushed after the employee before he made his escape. "We're meeting someone here," I told him. "Has a Monica Boatman showed up yet?"

"You're the first two today," the employee admitted, scratching his chin. "But I can let her know you've arrived if she shows up before we open. May I suggest the cliff viewpoint around the corner while you wait?"

I hadn't realized the island had cliffs. Everything so far had been fairly flat with the occasional hillside, so the premise of cliffs with a view drew me in. We may as well do some sightseeing while waiting for Monica. I checked my watch. She was officially late for the meeting. Great.

Letting the young man know we would return shortly, we made the brisk walk to the observation area. A slight wind ruffled my hair, and I inhaled the fresh smell of salt water as we inched closer to the cliff's edge. Joe stopped to look at an information deck displayed in a tall wooden frame beside an iron bench.

"Looks like this was one of the first areas to be built on the island," he said.

I looked toward the water, my eyes squinting against the bright sunlight. "I can see why. It's quite a view."

A shimmer of blue caught my eye. I swung around toward it, my stomach pitching. For a second, I thought I saw a rift open, but when I turned, there was nothing there. No interruption in the air, no rippling effect. Only the cliffs, the palm trees, and the ocean beneath.

And the ghost of an old man with a cane, shaking his fist at me.

"Oh, no," I whispered.

Joe must have not heard me, still busy with the history lesson, because he didn't reply. I gave the old man a wave, but he raised his fist higher, shaking it more violently. His lips opened, but no sound came out. The same as the ghost of the manager in the bank. He wore a pained expression, his gray, lifeless eyes crinkling at the corners.

From the look of his clothing, I'd estimate he had been dead for a long time. Maybe even since the first building erupted on this piece of land.

I took a tentative step forward. "Hi, sir. Do you need some help?"

Another silent opening of the mouth, this time wider and angrier. The man swung his cane at me as if to point. I looked back, seeing nothing there. When I returned to him, the man was gone.

"Did you see—"

The man appeared out of nowhere, making the words catch in my throat. His face was so close to mine that I could feel the cold of his ghostly body in my bones. I still couldn't hear him, but there was no mistaking it now. He was screaming.

"I don't understand," I said, my arms up in surrender. "I'm sorry."

He swung his cane again, this time to the right of us. When I faced the direction he pointed, I nearly screamed. The rift I thought I saw before was back, and it was larger than ever. The man continued to shout, warning me against it. I didn't know how to explain that I wasn't the one who should worry.

"Time to go," a booming voice said from within.

My father.

Shivering, I watched as the ghost continued to fight, the fear on his face palpable. My hands reached out, but he was dragged back, something pulling him from inside the rift, yanking him backward. Without a second thought, I ran after the ghost. My arms reached for him as I fought to get a grasp, even though I knew it made no sense. I couldn't hold a ghost. I couldn't help him.

And even if I could, did I want to?

Whatever reason my father had for pulling the ghost into the Underworld, it must have been valid.

"I do not belong to you!" the man screamed.

Figures. I could hear him now that it was too late. Half his body was already through the rift.

My eyes widened in horror. "Why do you want him?" I shouted.

"That is not your concern, daughter," my father said in return. "He is mine. They are all mine. They will always be mine."

The man shrieked, a terrible sound that reverberated through my body. Behind me, I heard Joe's voice as he ran for me. I didn't answer back. I didn't need to be saved from the Underworld, my father was not someone I feared. Perhaps that was my first mistake.

My second was to try to jump for the ghost as he was yanked into the closing rift. Before me, the air rippled and the darkness inside the rift lessened. A door closed as the ghost was swallowed whole right before my eyes. I leaped forward, realized too late that my feet had no purchase.

The cliffs ended, and I was stepping into thin air.

Two arms wrapped around my waist and jerked me away from the cliff's edge. I tripped and my back hit Joe's solid chest as we fell to the ground. My breath rushed from my lungs.

Joe's arms were still tightly wrapped around me when he said, "What happened here?"

"There was a ghost," I said, catching my breath. "My father wanted him for some reason, but he didn't want to go. It was horrible. The man, he was so in so much pain. I don't understand why Hades needs them. The spirits. He said they were his, all of them. What do you think he meant?"

Joe sat halfway up, pulling me with him. "It sounds bad, whatever it is. And I have more bad news."

I wiggled out of his embrace to face him.

"What?" I asked.

"Monica canceled. She said she can't risk talking to us and that if we knew what was good for us, we'd enjoy the rest of our vacation and stop pushing."

My brow furrowed. "That's odd. Why would she tell us to meet her and then bail?"

"I'm not sure. She called while you were ghost chasing, so I was a bit distracted," Joe admitted. "But she sounded afraid."

"Afraid? Of who?"

He shrugged. "I think maybe her husband. She mentioned that Fallon couldn't know that she talked to us." He raked a hand through his hair. "I don't know, Piper. She sounded really scared. Like he is a bad guy. A really bad guy."

The wheels turned in my head. The first time I spoke with Monica, she warned me against getting involved too. Perhaps Fallon Boatman wasn't only a sleazy businessman and a land tycoon. Was there a chance I was right and he was also an abusive husband?

And how far would someone like that go if he suspected his wife was having an affair as Collin did?

I looked past Joe toward the cafe. We may not have gotten any answers today, but I was certain of my next direction. We had to see what else we could find on Greenfield Industries and Fallon. Preferably before someone else turned up dead, maybe even Monica herself.

CHAPTER 19

F resh mango melted in my mouth as I watched the sun go down on the horizon. At my back, a clatter in the kitchen made me wince.

"I'm okay!" Joe yelled out.

I raised my hand to give him a thumbs up. In truth, I had barely noticed all the noise he was making while making dinner. Normally I'd be in there with him cutting up vegetables or giving whatever help the vampire needed, which often was very little since Joe was an expert cook. Seriously, for a paranormal who didn't need normal sustenance, he sure cooked a mean pasta primavera. But today I couldn't bring myself to pay attention and when Joe suggested I relax on the deck while he cooked, I jumped at the chance.

Sitting here now with the setting sun painting my face a deep shade of pink, I wanted to scream. My head was a jumble of random thoughts that didn't appear to be connected one bit. Not that I was some expert detective, but as of late, solving puzzles had become a new normal for me and I couldn't stand that this case had me stumped. Sure, back in Orchard Hollow, I had an entire village of help. If I truly wanted, I could call up Sheriff Romero. He'd be grumpy about it, but he would always offer his assistance if it meant we could bring a killer to justice. Then there was Cilia and her butt-kicking witch abilities. Not to mention my mom, who, while absent, was one of the most capable witches I knew.

But not on the island.

Here it was only Joe and me; Stella, if you counted her, which I didn't since she went off and vanished on us again. I was starting to think that my familiar met a ghost boyfriend and ran off with him.

A thought sent a shudder through me. What if Hades got to her?

I shook it off, refusing to give it a purchase. There was no way my father could have Stella Rutherford. If anyone was to give the God of Death a run for his money, it was my familiar. I chuckled. Chances were that if Hades did snatch her and dragged her into the Underworld, he'd throw her right back after a few minutes.

I stabbed a fork into another slice of mango and popped it into my mouth. Thoughts swirling, I worked to clear up my foggy brain, keeping track of each idea and categorizing it internally. There was so much information to sift through that I was having trouble figuring out what was important and what wasn't. A part of me considered what Monica Boatman said when she warned us about not looking further into the murders. Leaving this alone was likely the smartest solution, but it was also one that I couldn't accept.

Not when people were dying, and the police were nowhere close to finding the killer. Unless they were and we didn't know. Unlike with Romero, I had no clue what the cops on the island were up to, but I had been checking the news incessantly and hadn't seen anything thus far. I could only assume they were as stuck as I was.

I looked over my shoulder at Joe. At least I had him to help.

Polishing off the last of the fruit, I took stock of what we knew so far. We had two deaths that were seemingly unrelated. I didn't buy it. A missing woman. A wife who was afraid of her husband and had ties to both victims. A diamond earring and blueprints for a building site that wasn't actually being built on.

When I arranged the clues on the metaphorical table of my brain, there was only one common denominator, and his name was Fallon Boatman. He had a connection to everyone in the picture, either directly or indirectly. That couldn't be a coincidence. Not to mention the way Monica spoke about her husband gave me the creeps so I knew he wasn't a good guy. That and I couldn't get Joe's words out of my head. It could be our best bet was to forget all we knew and follow the money.

Fallon's money, to be precise.

I swung my legs over the lounge chair and stood up, heading inside. The air conditioning hit me in the face when I slid the glass door open and Collin's face flashed before me. I couldn't believe that he was here only a few days ago and now he was dead. Being a magnet for death was starting to really bother me. It wasn't that I minded being able to help bring justice to those with no voice but come on! Could I not take a proper vacation without two people dying on my watch? It seemed the answer was a fat resounding no.

I closed the door behind me, sliding onto a bar stool. "It smells amazing in here," I told Joe.

"Nearly ready. I hope you're hungry."

"Starved," I answered. My stomach growled in

agreement and we both laughed. "Hey, I've been thinking about what you said earlier."

Joe added more butter to the pan and tossed a handful of raw shrimp in to sizzle. His muscled back tensed and his ears perked up at my words. "If this is about the gold bikini, I was only kidding. Sort of."

"It's not," I said. "And that's not happening, so you should really get over it. But seriously, I think you had a point with what you said about Fallon."

Oil jumped off the pan and Joe covered it with a lid, taking it off the burner. In a bowl, he mixed a few ingredients that made the kitchen smell divine. My mouth watered as he said, "Could Stella follow the guy?"

"I'd have to find her first."

"Still no sign of her?" Joe asked. "Is that unusual?"

Reaching for an olive from the bowl on the counter, I tossed it in my mouth, chewing. "If we were back home, I'd say yes. The woman doesn't go a minute without bothering me, but I've never taken a vacation with a ghost. It's possible she needs a break from all things Piper."

"How could she?" Joe asked, looking extra offended.

I giggled. "Do you still have your laptop upstairs?"

"On the bed. Why?"

"I want to see if I can find anything on Fallon

online," I replied, already rising from the stool. "Unless you need my help with dinner."

A wave of the hand told me Joe was fine on his own and I bolted up the stairs, temporarily forgetting their danger. When I reached the bedroom, I slid onto the bed, the fluffy duvet swallowing me up. Powering up Joe's laptop, I pulled up a search bar and went straight to work. At first glance, there was nothing that stood out or caught my attention. Fallon didn't have much of a social media presence, and his professional profile had only a few blog posts and the same phone number he gave us before. I couldn't even find pictures of him and Monica together and that was after doing my best to online stalk the couple.

Greenfield Industries was a similar story. I found their company website and a few articles written about their latest builds, some good and some bad. It appeared that Collin was right and people were not all that happy with the developer's choice of real estate locations. Most of the areas the company built on caused some upset in the communities they belonged to; ones I couldn't argue since I could see their point. If someone built a massive resort in Orchard Hollow, I'd likely have a problem with it, too.

Other than those complaints, I barely found anything of use.

Scrolling through mindlessly, my eyes snagged on

the company's name in a forum site and I clicked on it instantly. A pop-up window instructing me to create an account blocked my view of the chat and after some frustration, I managed to sign up with a pseudonym. Spoiler alert. It was Stella's name which I figured she wouldn't mind since no one could track a dead woman.

The site logged me in and I doubled back to find the forum chat I originally saw. As I read the messages, goosebumps spread over my skin. My legs tensed on the bed and I pressed my face so close to the screen, I almost ended up inside it.

"Dinner is ready."

A yelp broke free of me and I jumped a little at the sound of Joe's voice from the doorway. He leaned on the frame, his arms folded over his chest. "Let me guess, you found something."

"Listen to this," I answered, scrolling up to the beginning of the chat. "According to a forum, this person used to work for Greenfield. User five six one one one four three."

"All right..." Joe said, dragging out the syllables.

I waved him over and waited until he was sitting beside me to continue. "I have a point, I promise. So this person claims they were fired for trying to speak up about the company's wrongdoings two years ago." I scrolled down, pointing to another chat bubble. "They say Greenfield is notoriously buying out property they can't build on. Then they get backers and early adopters for projects that either don't take flight, or worse."

"Worse how?"

Joe lowered to see the screen better, his curiosity peaked.

"We're talking about toxic waste issues, protected land, that kind of thing." I clicked on a gallery wall and expanded it on the screen. "This person even posted photos they took of the blueprints the company falsified. And look here—" I zoomed in on one in particular. "—Does that look familiar?"

Joe turned his head slightly and inspected the photo. His Adam's apple bobbed as he realized what he was looking at, the same reaction I had before. "Isn't that Turtle Cove?"

"Correct," I said. "Same blueprints we found in Robert's safety deposit box. You see something different on this set?"

Joe's finger tapped a row of thick lines spanning across the isle.

"That would be an old sewage system running under the entire piece of land. If Fallon was going to build a resort here, it would cost millions to clear the lines without toxic waste leaking into the soil and water. What do you think the chances are that he would do that?"

"I'm not sure."

I nodded. "According to user five six one one one four three, the chances are zero. They say that more often than not, Fallon either scrapped the project and kept all the investment money or went ahead with it despite the environmental concerns. Can you imagine if he were to build on Turtle Cove?"

"Lives would be at stake."

"So many lives," I agreed, my heart twisting. Eyes flicking to Joe, I asked, "Do you think Robert kept the blueprints because he was going to report the company? What if Fallon had him killed before he could?"

Taking the laptop from me, Joe skimmed the rest of the forum, the creases on his forehead deepening. He pulled up the images again to inspect them more and when he was done, he lowered the computer down and straightened his back. "If that's what happened, how come the whistleblower here is still alive?" he asked. "They clearly have enough to bring down the entire operation."

"I'm pretty sure it'd be impossible to find out who they are," I answered. "I had to hop through some hoops to set up an account and all the data appears to be encrypted. I'm no internet hacker, but I would assume your identity is well protected when you sign in. Besides, for all we know, user five six one one one four three is Robert Atlas. It could be his username."

Joe huffed out a long breath through his teeth. "That's a good point." He glanced at the laptop briefly. "This is not what I thought you'd find when I said to follow the money."

"I know."

The knot in my throat grew, and it made it difficult to breathe. I kept looking at the images in the forum and the sewage lines covering Turtle Cove. Fallon would have to be an absolute monster to build a resort over a toxic waste site. One wrong move and a pipe could burst, all those chemicals seeping out and tainting every form of life there. Sure, he would get caught before the resort opened, but what about all the poor iguanas that use it as a home?

Weren't they an endangered species of sorts?

I didn't know much about island laws, but I would assume this type of disregard for life had all kinds of jail sentences attached to it. How could any amount of money be worth it?

And yet it likely was for some people. It was always shocking to find out how much of an effect money had on people.

I closed the lid of the laptop and shimmied myself up the bed, sitting cross-legged near Joe. In my chest, my runner's heart built with tension. Meeting his questioning gaze, I pushed my hair back with my hands and steadied my uneven breath. "Do you still have the business card Fallon gave us?"

"Downstairs, I think," Joe said.

I pressed my lips into a tight line. "Good. I believe I'd like to speak to him about investing in property, after all."

CHAPTER 20

Greenfield Industries smelled and looked like money. It had all the telltale signs of luxury, or at least the appearance of such. If the palm trees lining the long driveway leading to the glass mansion weren't enough, they also had them in gargantuan planters all throughout the lobby of the office. Sleek cream couches sat around the wide-open space with polished marble side tables next to them. On the walls, sixty-inch screens played loops of three-dimensional architectural structures and graphics of reviews from happy clients. There were even a few pictures added for extra flair.

I noticed none of the people in the photos looked like victims of toxic waste shock.

A woman's sing-song voice echoed through the empty lobby, drawing me in. Joe and I turned in unison to a pristinely put-together assistant behind the longest reception desk I had ever seen. This thing must have been the size of a small ship. Made entirely of glass, it sparkled as the overhead chandelier reflected rainbow-colored rays across it. There was no way the poor woman could get any work done with all that flare in her eyes.

I nudged Joe in the ribs and he stifled a laugh as we padded across the shiny tile floor toward the desk. When we approached, the woman flashed us a brilliant smile, lowered her headset to whisper, "Be right with you," and pointed to one couch. She then proceeded to ignore us entirely for a good fifteen minutes.

When she was done, I had zoned out and was staring into a blank space on the wall, completely missing her calling us back over.

"We're up," Joe whispered, waking me from my coma.

We hurried to the desk, its shadow looming over us. The woman rose a little off her chair to glare down at us from her throne above. "Welcome to Greenfield Industries. Do you have an appointment?"

Shouldn't she have asked us that before she made us wait? I shook off the negative attitude.

"Fallon told us to stop by anytime," Joe said. "We're looking to invest and were hoping to discuss a few prospects with him."

A storm brewed behind the woman's hazel eyes. Was I imagining things, or did she seem uncomfortable at the mention of an investment? Could she be another employee who knew the dirty secrets this place kept behind closed doors? I wanted to reach over the thick desk and shake her for answers. Instead, I forced the edges of my lips to curl up into a smile and said, "Beautiful office you have here."

Whatever I saw before vanished and the woman flashed her teeth at me again. This time she smiled so openly that I could see her molars.

"Only the best for our clients," she said cheerfully. "You said Mr. Boatman personally invited you?"

I nodded.

"Very well. Let me see if he's available."

The woman put her headset back on and we were back to waiting on the couch. At this rate, I'd die of old age before we saw Fallon. The man was better guarded than the Mona Lisa.

After what felt like a lifetime, we were beckoned forth again, this time being led through two frosted glass doors around one side of the reception desk. The woman's four-inch heels clicked on the tile floor as she hurried toward an office at the far end of the hallway.

She moved so fast I worried she might slide across the slippery floor and break a leg, but she moved expertly, as someone who was used to making this trek from the front. She reminded me of a figure skater with her long legs and straight-backed gait.

When we reached another door, the woman knocked on it lightly. "Mr. Boatman, I have..." She turned to us, horror on her face.

I fought back a laugh. In all her exaggerated professionalism, she had forgotten to ask for our names.

"Piper and Joe," I whispered. "From the restaurant."

The woman repeated what I said through a crack in the door, then proceeded to swing it open and gesture inside with a rigid hand. I half-bowed awkwardly before stepping in, Joe hot on my heels. As we entered, the door closed behind us like we were in a haunted house carnival ride. I yipped forward for fear it might quite literally hit my behind.

We stepped further into the office, the light streaming in from the wall-to-wall windows spanning across the corner office blinding me temporarily. Sitting at a mahogany table and limned in light was Fallon Boatman. The developer tracked our steps as we neared him to sit in the two chairs pulled out for guests. His forehead was creased with lines and there were fresh drops of sweat collecting in the crevices. Today, Fallon appeared a lot less full of himself, and if I had to guess, I'd say he was nervous.

But why?

There was nothing to imply that we were here for anything but investing. Joe and I were careful not to say too much, and we both kept our features relaxed and warm. I even feigned excitement as I lowered to sit, which didn't help put Fallon at ease in the slightest.

"Piper, Joe!" Fallon finally exclaimed. "Pleasure to see you both again. I see you decided to take me up on my offer."

A bead of sweat rolled down his forehead, and he brushed it off before it hit his eye. *What was going on with him?*

I shifted my weight in the chair. "Thank you for seeing us on such short notice."

"Nonsense. I'm always happy to speak with potential investors."

Flashes of the forum chat drifted before me. *I bet you are.* My throat itched at the need to get straight into why we came, but Joe intercepted before I ruined everything.

"The more we thought about it, the more we realized how much we love the island," he said. "It would be great to have a place to visit. Something that's ours, you know?"

The words seemed to please Fallon, because he finally relaxed his tight shoulders and leaned back in the office chair. "I couldn't agree more. Have you had a chance to look at our available locations? We have a few pre-builds you might be interested in."

Joe and I exchanged a quick glance, which Fallon caught. He pulled on his silk tie, the motion leaving a red line across his tanned skin.

"Is there a problem?" Fallon asked.

"Not a problem, no," I quickly corrected. "After what Robert said, we had a chance to visit Turtle Cove and we have to say we really love that place. It's a shame you're not actually building there because we would be willing to invest quite a bit in that location."

Another tug of the tie. "Yes, yes. A shame."

"See, Robert was pretty clear on the location. Very odd, wouldn't you say?"

A spark of recognition behind Fallon's eyes gave me pause. He knew what I was getting at and he was playing along. I knew it! Our theory about the blueprints was right on the money. Fallon was a greedy son of a latte and I would bet my life that for the right price, he'd sell us a fraction of his soul. The prospective site on Turtle Cove wasn't advertised because of the legal ramifications of building over the sewage lines, not to mention the endangered species living there. But that wasn't to say that the slimeball in front of us wouldn't cash in on it on the sly.

I nudged Joe with my foot under the table, hoping he caught my drift.

He did, thankfully.

"As Piper said, that site has our full attention," Joe said. He rested an elbow on the table, making sure to flash his designer watch from back in his rich-boy lawyer days. "We have a generous amount to work with and were really hoping to put it somewhere we are passionate about."

The glint in Fallon's eyes made my stomach turn. The greasy developer gravitated toward Joe like a bug to a lava lamp. His cheeks reddened from the pressure of the desk on his abdomen, but he kept pushing closer. "How generous are we talking about here?"

I absolutely despise you.

Battling the urge to roll my eyes, my lips twitched a little as I worked my jaw. "Very," I said.

Keeping his attention on me, Fallon reached into a desk drawer and pulled out a black file folder. He put it on the desk, slowly sliding it toward us. My heart pitter-pattered as the man flipped open the folder and I got ready to accuse him of trying to fraud us out of money. When I glanced at the printout inside the folder, my excitement deflated.

I double-checked to make sure I wasn't mistaken. "This isn't Turtle Cove."

The pictures in the printout looked nothing like the isle I visited. The more I studied it, the more I realized it wasn't even on this island, since the vegetation in some of the color images didn't match anything we'd seen since we landed. I scratched the back of my head, confused.

"As I mentioned," Fallon insisted, "Turtle Cove is not an option."

"But Robert—"

Fallon slammed a fist on the desk. "Robert shouldn't have said anything to you. It is no longer available."

"But it was before?" I asked.

Face paling, the developer shrank away from us, pulling the folder back with him. His ears reddened and I could see there was plenty he wanted to say but was trying to be professional. "Look, I'm sorry to have wasted your time. There was some miscommunication. We don't have what you're looking for." His eyes darted to the door. Something shifted in the developer and for the first time since we walked in, I recognized what it was. Fear. Fallon Boatman was afraid.

I pulled away from the desk to give the man some space. The sweat rolled off him in waves and he continued to tug on his tie like it was suffocating him.

Motioning at Joe, I nudged for him to follow suit and he adapted instantly. The serious expression he wore before vanished, replaced by a calm demeanor and a relaxed jaw. This was no longer an interrogation. Something had the developer spooked. I wanted to make sure he knew we weren't a threat.

"Maybe we misheard," I said sweetly. "We'll gladly take a look at other options if you have them."

Fallon dipped his chin to glance at the folder in his hands. He held it so tight, the paper had begun to tear. When I reached for it, he yanked it away, his head shaking. "No, I can't let you do that," he said, shoving the folder back in the drawer. "It wouldn't be right."

"How come?" Joe asked.

The man crumpled before us. His head dropped into his hands and he raked his fingers through his hair over and over. His shoulders shook as he looked up at us through bushy brows. Hand slipping over his face, he scrubbed his mouth, eyes wetting.

"I-I can't lie to Robert's friends. It isn't right," he blurted out. "So much of what I've done isn't right."

There was a half-full glass of water on the desk and I slid it towards him. Fallon thanked me with a tip of the chin, downing the remainder of the glass. His gaze stayed on the floor. "I'm a terrible person."

"What did you do?" Joe asked.

For a moment, I was certain the man was about to

confess to killing Robert and Collin. Without him seeing, I slipped out my phone and opened the voice record application. Before I could start it, Fallon spoke again, shattering my hopes.

"The business is folding. We're going under."

"Sorry, what?" I asked.

Fallon's fingers intertwined, and he stretched his arms over the table. "I'm closing the company. We've gone bankrupt," he said.

"But the investors, the building sites, your website..."

"All lies," Fallon said sternly. "A facade to get people to give us money. I am ashamed to admit that my practices were less than honest."

Some might say they're illegal.

The creases were back on Fallon's forehead, deep gashes that aged him considerably. "What Robert told you about Turtle Cove was the truth. We did plan to open a resort there, despite circumstances that would have made it unethical. But after what happened to Robert, I couldn't go through with it. Life is too short. I had to stop what I was doing before it ate me up inside. That's why I sold that site and others like it."

"You should ask him about the federal bureau sniffing around."

My body jerked at the sound of Stella's voice behind me. Careful not to make sudden movements, I turned over my shoulder, the ghost hovering a few feet away. Where had she been? And what did Stella mean about the feds being after Fallon?

I arched an eyebrow questioningly.

"He didn't sell those sites out of the goodness of his heart," the ghost said. "Ask him about his friend on the force."

Trusting my familiar, I crossed my arms and deadpanned on Fallon. "What about your cop friend?"

Next to me, Joe stirred in his seat but stayed quiet.

Fallon's eyes widened. "How do you know about that?" He shook his head. "It doesn't matter. Yes, I may have had a little warning from a good friend that I should be careful, but believe me, Robert's death is what did it. I couldn't keep going down this dark path. It was a bad move. I can't even begin to say how sorry I am for the things we did."

I didn't believe a word this sleazeball ball was saying. The look of disgust on Joe's face told me he agreed one hundred percent.

"Awful little man," Stella echoed from behind me.

You said it.

"What's going to happen to all the people who invested in your fraudulent schemes?" I asked.

The developer winced. "The company is bankrupt," he said. That was all the answer I needed. The poor people he scammed were never going to see a penny of their hard-earned money. Fallon's face scrunched, and it made my hate for him deepen. "I really am so sorry for everything."

Doubtful. I looked at him venomously. "How can you live with yourself?"

"It's why I had to stop," Fallon answered.

Nerves boiling over, I stomped out my anger and pulled the chair out, rising to stand. Fallon mumbled something about his wife not finding out, and I let it go. I had nothing more to say to the worm. Whatever idea I'd had of the developer being behind the murders was gone without a trace—this was not the killer. Fallon was nothing more than a miserable, money-hungry jerk.

Did he do a whole lot of bad? Yes.

Was he the most despicable human being I had met in a while? Also yes.

But did I think he had the motive to kill Robert and Collin? Not in the slightest.

Leaving the worm to wallow in self-pity, I waited until Joe stood up and stormed out of the office. The woman at the reception desk eyed us warily as we marched out. I caught a flash of guilt in her expression. Ignoring my need to tell her what I thought of the place she worked in, I pushed out of the building with a huff. The hot afternoon air slapped me in the face and I gritted my teeth, stomping to the car. When I reached it, I turned around, waiting for Stella to emerge.

"How did you know about the cop that tipped him off?" I asked the ghost.

She smirked. "You're not the only one who is a detective savant."

"Holy coffee bean, will you let that go already?" I slapped my thighs in frustration. "This entire time, you've been investigating Fallon."

"Sure, let's go with that," Stella said. "Not why I'm here, though."

I crinkled my nose at her. What other reason would my familiar have to show up at Greenfield, of all places, if it wasn't to give us the scoop on what she found out? "All right, I'll bite. Why are you here?"

"To tell you that you need to get back to the villa," the ghost said. "Someone left you a message you're not going to like."

CHAPTER 21

'Back off or you're next.'

I read the note over, my hands trembling as I pulled it off the front door. A deep-rooted fear clawed at my heart and I had trouble shaking it off. The fact that the note was stabbed to the door with a large kitchen knife probably had a lot to do with it.

"We're leaving," Joe announced. "Today."

"Are you—"

He cut me off, ushering me into the villa. Before closing the door and locking it, he checked up and down the street as though the person who left the warning was hanging around waiting for us to get back. "Look, Piper, this is getting out of hand. We can plan for another trip later, but for now, I'd feel a lot more comfortable if we got an earlier flight."

"Do you really think we're in danger?"

"I'm not sure," Joe said. "But two people are dead and as much as I know you want to help figure out what happened, we have a target on our backs now."

I looked at the note in my hands. "This person doesn't know who they're dealing with."

"Piper, we are not going to be out here going all paranormal on a killer. No matter what happens, it's important that we keep our abilities hidden from humans. You know that." He reached for my hand, holding it in his. "It's even more important that I know you are safe, and I no longer believe that. Please tell me you understand where I'm coming from."

As much as I didn't want to admit it, I did. This was supposed to be a vacation and a chance for Joe and me to relax, to put all the horrible things we'd been through lately behind us. Mostly, it was supposed to make me feel normal and not like my entire life was intertwined with death. So far, it had been the complete opposite. Not knowing who killed Robert and Collin was going to weigh on my mind for years to come, perhaps even forever, but it wasn't worth the risk. And it certainly wasn't worth losing Joe over.

I gave his hands a squeeze. "You're right. We should leave."

"Great. I'm going upstairs to see if I can switch our flight home."

Placing a soft peck on my cheek, Joe walked up the stairs and disappeared from view. My fingers crumpled the note, and I tossed it in the trash, closing the lid with a bang. After downing two bottles of water from the fridge, I opened the trash can and fished out the note, unfolding it on the island.

The handwriting was strange. It appeared to be written purposely messy. Like someone used their non-dominant hand to scribble the message to avoid detection. I remember doing something similar when I was a kid to leave secret messages to Gran in the house. The plan was to make her think I was a ghost with a message from the beyond, one that often included giving me extra cookies after dinner. It seemed the afterlife followed me even then.

I tried to find some clue in the note in front of me, coming up empty. If there was anything on the piece of paper that told me who wrote the note, I wasn't seeing it. After twenty minutes of racking my brain with little success, I gave up, tossing the note away again.

Footsteps echoed from upstairs as Joe came back down.

"Any luck?" I asked.

He shrugged. "Sort of. The soonest we can leave is tomorrow night on the red eye."

"Well, that's something." I glanced up the stairs. "I guess we should pack. It's a real shame we have to go."

"It is. But hey, like I said, we will plan another trip. One that doesn't include any murders."

I didn't have the heart to tell him that knowing my luck that would never be the case. Instead, I followed Joe back to the bedroom so we could pack our suitcases and have our final dinner at the villa. The exhaustion of the last few days was finally taking hold of me, and I vowed to make it an early night. If we were going to be up to catch a late flight tomorrow, I wanted to get up early and enjoy the last bit of island sunshine while we were here. Even sneak in a swim. I was sure going to miss that water.

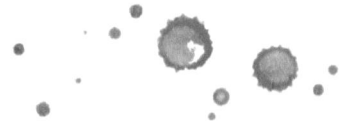

I awoke with a start. Outside the bedroom, the sky was pitch black with a dusting of stars, letting me know it was later than I thought. Beside me, Joe slept, his chest rising and falling with deep breaths. My throat felt like sandpaper and I reached for a glass on the nightstand, only to find it empty. I must have drunk it before falling asleep.

Next to the glass, my phone screen showed the time. I groaned. Three in the morning.

Slipping out quietly so I didn't wake up Joe, I padded from the room and went downstairs. My palm felt along the wall until I found a light-switch and I flicked it, heading for the fridge. A gray face jumped out at me. I yelped, stumbling back a few steps, my back colliding with the side of the island.

"Geez! Stella!"

The ghost flipped her long ponytail over a slender shoulder. "Sorry."

"What are you doing skulking around in the dark?"

"Same as you."

I doubted that very much, but didn't say so. Ghosts didn't have the same needs as those of us still breathing. The chances that Stella couldn't sleep were slim to none. I appreciated her solidarity in keeping me company, though, considering that she'd all but ditched me for most of the trip.

Skirting around her, I reached into the fridge for the water filter and poured myself a large glass.

"Are you really leaving?" Stella asked.

I grimaced. "Guess so. Joe is worried about staying,

and I can't really blame him. Don't worry, there will be other vacations."

"That's not it."

"Then what is it?"

Flicking her eyes past my shoulder, the ghost floated closer to the island, her transparent body inches from mine. She placed her hands on the marble, concentrating on making the physical connection with the cold stone. "You haven't found the killer," she finally said.

"I know. But I'm sure the police can handle it."

The ghost quirked a brow. "Doubtful."

"What's really bothering you, Stella?"

"Well, don't you want to know what happened?" she asked, her fingers curling into tight little fists. "Solving these cases, that's kind of our thing now, isn't it?"

I chuckled. I supposed it was. My shoulders hiked up. I opened my mouth to convince Stella that leaving was for the best when a garish face in the backyard caught my attention. Goosebumps spread over my skin and the hair on the rear of my neck stood on end. I gestured with my head toward the glass doors until Stella caught my drift.

"Oh," she said nonchalantly. "We have a visitor."

Glaring at us through the doors was Collin, or his ghost, I supposed. Unlike Stella, he was in terrible shape, his body twisted awkwardly like he forgot how to be properly put together. He took a floating step forward, his one leg bent at an odd angle and drifting behind him. If I had to guess, I'd say Collin was stuck in the same position that he had died in.

Strange.

"What do you think he wants?" Stella asked.

As she did, Collin opened his mouth wide, but no sound came out. He tried again, saying things we couldn't hear or understand. I left my post at the island and tip-toed toward the back of the villa, reaching for the door handles.

"Are you sure that's wise?" Stella asked at my back.

I slid the doors wide open. "What can he really do?"

I immediately regretted that statement.

As soon as the doors were open, Collin's ghostly body rushed for me. My skin crawled as he shoved through me then back again, his mouth silent speaking the entire time. I shivered, brushing off my arms and jumping from foot to foot. "Can you not?" I hissed out.

Collin didn't reply. He kept trying to talk. I had no idea what he was saying since I couldn't understand him. Memories of the man at the cliffs came back to me and I scanned the backyard for signs of a rift, but there was none.

"I'm sorry, I can't hear you," I told Collin.

His aggravation was written all over his face. He tried again with the same results.

I shrugged. "Still nothing." Then, turning to Stella, asked, "Why can't I hear him but I can hear you?"

"No clue," my familiar said. "But I can't hear him either, so there's that. It could be the island."

Or my father. I didn't want to say it out loud, but I had the distinct feeling that whatever was happening with the rifts was causing this. Things had been changing lately and it upset me that I couldn't explain them. It also upset me that I could suddenly see ghosts other than Stella because who needed that in their lives? But that was neither here nor there, so I chose to leave it alone.

Hovering a foot in front of me, Collin made a motion at the top of his head. I shook my head. "Still nothing."

His arms wheeled, and he stormed off in the direction of the villa next door.

"Should we follow him?" I asked Stella.

My familiar was already on the other side of our property line, her expression unreadable. "Obviously, Piper."

Glancing back inside for Joe, I turned on my heels and rushed after the two spectres ruining my last night on the island. Around me, the sound of waves lapping the shore filled the air as I stepped over the low stone-lined path and snuck into the adjoining backyard. The Atlas villa loomed behind me, a reminder of death.

I pushed the thought out of my mind and concentrated on keeping up with Collin, who led us to the garden gnome in the yard. Eyes landing on Stella, I asked, "What's this now?"

"I think he wants you to pick it up."

Sure enough, Collin's index finger was pointing directly at the gnome. Following the instruction, I bent down and snatched the little fella from the grass. The gnome was heavier than I expected, and it took a bit of effort for me to raise it. I held it up to Collin. "Now what?"

Before he could reply, something fell out of the bottom of the statue and clattered to the ground. My chin dipped. I dove to catch whatever it was, my knees sliding on the grass. Clumsily, I searched the ground, my fingers wrapping around a small metal stick.

"What is it?" Stella asked.

I held it up, the light of the moon bouncing off the metal. My heart leaped into my throat. "A flash drive," I told my familiar. "From a security camera."

CHAPTER 22

"Did it work?" Joe yelled, his voice muffled, head stuck behind the wide screen television in the living room.

I watched the screen come to life with a black-and-white image. Cords stuck out from the television and fed into Joe's laptop, a setup he worked all morning to figure out so we could see the footage on the flash drive. Now, sitting with my feet tucked under me on the couch, I almost wished we hadn't. Dread crawled up my body as I watched the image sharpen the more Joe tinkered with the wires.

"It's up!" I told him.

Climbing out, Joe settled on the couch beside me and dragged the laptop onto his lap. Stella floated a few feet from the screen and furrowed her brow in concentration. Or, at least, I assumed her brow was furrowed, since there was no way to tell considering how much work Stella had done to reverse even the smallest sign of aging.

Shooting me a quick nod, Joe pressed play, and the video came to life. The sound bar below the television crackled, and I sank into the cushions of the couch, my head swirling.

"That's the inside of the villa next door," I said. "Why is there a camera in there? And how did Collin know about it?"

Sure enough, the Atlas villa was unmistakable. The screen was divided into four, each rectangle showing a different part of the home. I instantly recognized the steep stairs that mirrored ours and the bedroom I found the safety deposit key in. There was a timestamp at the bottom right corner and my eyes narrowed on it. The night of Robert's death.

A shiver tripped my spine.

Peeling his gaze from the screen, Joe looked around the room. "You don't think he had one here, too?"

"Ew," Stella remarked. "A peeping Tom. How blasé."

I scoffed. "Blasé is not the word I'd use. Was Collin recording his guests without their knowledge?"

No one said a word. The thought of us, Joe and me, being recorded the entire time we were vacationing was horrifying, not to mention all types of illegal. The way I felt about Collin morphed, a dark disgust forming in my gut. A flash of his ghost being sucked into the rift to be dealt justice by my father made my head spin. I shook it off. I couldn't go down that route. Whatever gross things Collin did, I would not allow the darkness to overcome me. I was not my father, and I did not wish harm upon anyone, creep or not.

I focused my attention back on the screen, relieved that the others did the same. No one wanted to think about the cameras possibly planted in our villa, but I was certain Joe would scour for them later. And I was even more certain that I'd be letting the police know what Collin was up to while he was alive.

Checking the footage, I sighed in relief. At least there didn't appear to be cameras in the bathroom.

The footage lagged and the crackling sound continued to pour through the speakers. Joe pressed a button to lower the volume slightly, but I stopped him before he muted the entire thing; there may be something we needed to hear on here. A shadow passed by the rectangle showing the back door and we all leaned in to see better.

I gasped as Carla entered the scene. "Do you think that was the last time she was seen?"

"Probably," Joe answered.

We watched in agitated silence as the door opened again. My jaw slacked, the muscles too shocked to hold it up.

"Plot twist," Stella said with a grin.

Entering the villa after Carla was Monica Boatman. She slid the glass doors shut behind her and followed Carla toward the kitchen, the one that was a replica of ours. I kept my eyes trained on the women, mouthing, "This must have been right after Carla left the restaurant," out of the side of my mouth.

I expected the women to say something to give us an idea of what happened to Carla. What I didn't expect was what happened next. Monica walked up to Carla, her gait predatory and hungry. The women locked eyes and the jaw I tried so hard to keep up, smashed to the ground.

"Are they?"

"Making out?" I said. "Definitely. Big time."

Stella inched closer to the screen like she was attempting to be one with it. "Told you. Plot twist."

"Well, this is unexpected," Joe said.

I leaned forward, resting my chin in my hands. My elbows dug into my knees and I averted my eyes to give the women on the screen privacy. Unlike Stella, I didn't need to be part of the love affair. This truly was very unexpected. My eyes widened to saucers. "You know what this means, right?" I asked the room. "The entire time that Collin thought Monica was coming here to see Robert, she was actually with Carla. The women were having an affair behind their husbands' backs."

"I wonder if Collin installed the cameras to catch Robert and Monica together, but saw this instead," Joe mused.

"Hmm, possibly. The bank manager did say that he was trying to get more money out of Robert for the villa. Maybe he planned to blackmail him to get it."

Joe puckered his lips. "But Robert died before he could. It's a good theory."

The sound of a door slamming shut made us both jump. Our heads turned to the backyard to find it empty. The sound came from the television. We swung back around, our teeth splitting as we watched Robert enter the villa.

"I knew it!" the man screamed. "Are you kidding me, Carla? How long has this been going on for?"

Oh, no.

Carla pulled away from Monica and faced her husband. There was fear etched on her face, but it vanished the second Monica took her hand for support. "Are you really surprised?" the second woman asked. "Maybe if you didn't spend all your time working and actually paid attention to your wife, you'd see how amazing she is."

"No one is talking to you!" Robert roared.

"Robert, please," Carla begged. "Calm down."

Her husband paced the length of the living room, then back again. His fingers twitched at his sides and I could feel his anger through the screen. Fuming, he spun around to face the women, his eyes narrowed. "I can't believe you'd humiliate me this way. After everything I did for you."

"Everything you did?" Monica asked with a scoff.

"I told you to shut up!" Robert screamed.

Leaving Monica's side, Carla rushed over to her husband, her hands clasped at her chest. "Robert, let's talk this out. There is no need to get so worked up. We can figure it all out together."

"Oh, we'll talk it out all right," the man seethed. He reached into his pants pocket and pulled out his phone. "I'm going to have a nice talk with Fallon right now. See what he has to say about all of it."

My eyes flashed to Monica at the same time hers met Carla's. The women nodded to each other, and the pit in my stomach grew. *No, no, no.* It was foolish of me to beg them not to do what I knew was coming next; it had already been done. I watched in horror as Carla pushed Robert, knocking the phone out of his hand and him onto the floor. She jumped on his back, her knee buried into his spine.

While Robert screamed and tried to free himself, Monica jumped for something on the wall.

"The net!" I shouted, pointing.

On the wall behind the couch hung a large fishing net. It was secured by two long screws, the holes I saw when I first set foot next door. With ease, Monica yanked the net down and the screws went flying, rolling somewhere under the couch. My palm pressed tightly to my lips.

Next to me, Joe stiffened, wrapping one arm around me as we watched the terrible scene unfold. One second Monica was by the couch and Carla wrestled her husband on the floor. The next, the net was wrapped around his neck and the women were pulling with all their force. I shut my eyes, unable to see what happened next. Luckily, Joe shut the recording down before we were all scarred for life.

"Hey!" Stella exclaimed. "I was watching that."

Some of us more than others, I supposed.

Nerves tingling, I peeled one eye open, then the other. Joe was fumbling with the laptop, pushing buttons frantically.

"What are you doing?" I asked.

He barely looked at me. "Making a copy," he replied. "I'm going to take this to the police."

With that, he got up and started for the front door. Turning to glance at me over his shoulder, he said, "Lock the doors. Finish packing. We're leaving the second I'm back."

And he was gone.

"Dramatic much?" Stella asked as the door shut.

I blinked slowly. "He isn't wrong. Come on, keep me company while I get the bags ready."

"Did you hear what they said at the end?"

I paused, my butt halfway off the couch and halfway on.

"The recording," Stella explained. "Did you hear what Monica said in the end?"

"No. I was trying not to hear any of it."

"Press play."

I started to object, but the ghost gave me an exasperated look, which meant I better do what she said or I'd never hear the end of it. Annoyed, I pushed play and prayed that the worst of what happened that night was over. The screen was silent save for the sound of dragging somewhere near the back doors.

"Rewind," Stella instructed. I did as she asked until she told me to stop. "There! Listen."

My ears perked as Carla's voice filled the room.

"Oh, dear lord, what did we do?" she asked between sobs. "We have to call the police. We have to tell someone."

"Babe, stop," Monica commanded. She reached for Carla's shoulders, giving them a little squeeze. "You have to hide. We will figure this out, but you can't be here."

"But Robert—"

"Is gone," Monica said. The lack of emotion in her tone made me freeze over. "I need you to get it together. Go get Robert's bike and meet me outside. I know somewhere you can go."

Carla trembled. "What about Robert?"

"I'll take care of it. Now, go!"

The recording shut off with a click. My mind raced as the pieces slowly came together. Collin knew what happened, and he'd died for it. Since Carla was on the run, it only made sense that Monica killed him too, to hide their secret. Geez. The Boatmans were two peas in a pod. Both of them thinking only of themselves. My blood ran cold.

"Where do you think she's hiding?" Stella asked.

I knew the answer without having to think about it. "The tracks we saw at Turtle Cove. How much do you want to bet they were from the bike Monica mentioned?"

Not wasting a moment, Stella floated past me, heading for the exit. She nudged her head in the direction of the exit, waiting for me to join. I didn't bother arguing because we both knew there was no way I would stay put. Sending a quick text to Joe, I hoped he would get it in time and not be too upset with me for doing what I was about to do.

I grabbed the keys for the villa and stormed out the front door, locking it behind me. It was time to finish this.

CHAPTER
23

Turtle Cove wasn't as busy as it was the last time I was here. There was only one other couple on the boat ride over and when we docked, I realized we were the only people here. Seeing my confusion, the captain of the boat informed me that the restaurant and bar don't open until noon, which is when the herd of people usually arrive. His smile widened as he told us to enjoy our private island.

The couple was ecstatic. Me, not so much.

I'd have preferred witnesses if my hunch was right about Carla.

Leaving the couple to explore the beach, I savored the sensation of the cool ocean breeze against my skin as I rolled up the hem of my loose pants, preparing for a brisk walk. The rhythmic sound of waves crashing against the shore helped calm my nerves as I set off down the familiar path I took before.

Passing the quaint restaurant nestled among palm trees, I quickened my pace, a sense of urgency tugging at my thoughts. Monica's presence on this trail the last time lingered in my mind, pushing me to move forward. With each stride, I stole glances at my phone, hoping for a message from Joe, but only silence greeted me. Perhaps he was too busy with the police, unaware of my attempts to reach out.

As I pressed forward, Stella trotted a few steps ahead, her senses attuned to any potential threats lurking amidst the foliage. Her presence offered a reassurance and an acknowledgment that I wasn't entirely alone here. With Stella by my side, I forged ahead, determined to find the truth that lay deep inside the jungle.

We made the brisk walk down the winding trail and I battled the jungle-like surroundings, swatting away palm leaves and flies. Up ahead, the sound of water crashing down made me speed up. We were so close now. I bent down to avoid a low-hanging branch, ducking under it to make my way toward the area I saw the tracks in.

When I reached them, I skidded to a stop.

"We're here," I told Stella.

The ghost looped around a palm tree to come join me. She studied the tracks, bending low to the ground and following their trajectory. "Where do you think they lead?"

"Probably over there," I told her, pointing to a rock formation to the left of the waterfall.

Stella stretched to see past the pond and the row of iguanas on the rocks surrounding it. "Are you planning to swim across?"

"Obviously not," I told the ghost. "Let's see if we can walk around the pond and sneak in the back."

We cut through overgrown vegetation, walking for what seemed like miles. Above us, the sun beat down heavily, not a cloud in the sky today. Sweat rolled off me and I felt my feet swelling in my running shoes. I probably should have worn sandals as Stella suggested, but these were the only shoes I hadn't packed yet and we were low on time. Despite the current mission we were on, I still had every hope of enjoying some time at the beach before our flight tonight. All I wanted was to check if my suspicions were right and confirm that Carla was alive. After that, I was done.

The police could handle the rest of this mess.

My fingers twitched as I walked, my magic sitting silently beneath my skin. Waiting. Out of the corner of my eye, I saw Stella look at me approvingly and I smiled. She was right, this was kind of our thing now.

We reached the side of the waterfall and I rolled my gaze over it with a low whistle. It was much taller than it looked from the other side of the pond, the stream of the water much stronger. More dangerous. I exchanged a quick look with Stella, then got to work inspecting the area for tire tracks. As suspected, the bike tracks were all over the ground, mixed in with shuffled footprints. There were a few iguana prints too, but the cute little guys were all gathered on the opposite side, where the sun streamed through the foliage to form a bright circle.

Following them, I walked the path with the tracks around a large boulder, using my hand for balance. From across the pond, the rock formation appeared to be stacked closely together, but now that I stood here, I could see an opening between them. A cavern entrance of sorts.

My chest constricted. "Should we?"

The ghost was through the crack and in the deep, swallowing darkness of the cavern before I even finished asking. Steeling my spine, I stepped in behind her. It took a second for my eyes to adjust to the dim light. In here, the space wasn't as tight as it appeared from the outside, and I could see remnants of a human presence all around. A leather satchel was propped against a rocky wall, its contents spilling out. I noticed several sweaters, pants, and other articles of clothing perfect for layering. Scattered on the floor were empty bottles of water and takeout food containers. In the center of the small cave was a sleeping bag, a portable heater, and a stack of books.

Carla was camping out here.

My eyes caught on a manila envelope under one of the books and I darted toward it, picking it up quickly. I yanked out the papers inside, my eyes running over the text to memorize it.

"What is it?" Stella asked.

I flipped through the pages again, to be sure. "Looks like a copy of a prenup signed by Monica and Fallon." I checked the next few pages. "And a lease on a rental property under Monica's name in the Grand Caymans."

Turning my phone on, I took pictures of the pages and tucked everything back into the envelope, returning it to the spot under the book.

"Why do you think that stuff is here?" Stella asked.

"I'm not sure," I replied. "But if I had to guess, I'd say that Monica couldn't simply leave her husband. According to the prenup, she'd lose everything. If Fallon were to find out about the affair, her entire life would be over. Unless..."

The ghost stopped moving. "Unless what?"

"Well, I was thinking that we didn't suspect Fallon

until we spoke with Monica. Do you think her plan was to frame him for Robert's murder, then hightail it out of here?"

"Without Carla?"

My shoulders shimmied. "Or with her. We should tell Joe and the cops about this. They'll want to come back here. Hopefully they're not too late and the two haven't left the island yet."

Giving the cave one last look around, I shoved my phone in my pocket and walked to the opening. The bright light from outside blinded me briefly and as I stepped out, it took me a second to orient myself. I started to walk back to the trail, but something hard slammed into the back of my head. My eyes, still slightly blurry, unfocused. I grunted as my knees hit the ground.

"Piper!" Stella yelled out.

It sounded muffled and wrong. I pressed a hand to my head where I felt the hit and it pulled away wet. "Is that blood?" I asked a second before the world spun in circles, then went completely black.

CHAPTER 24

Was I dead? My head throbbed, a constant hammering in my ears keeping me from being able to focus my eyes. I blinked the black dots swarming my vision, a thick knot forming in my throat.

The smell of iron filled my nostrils as I tried to stand up, but my body was too heavy to move. I wiggled my fingers and toes, a tingle shooting up my extremities. *Not dead, then.*

Around me, a darkness deeper than night swallowed me whole, enveloping me against my will and drowning out my senses. What happened? Flashes of the last few moments before I passed out passed before me, each image vivid and unsettling. I groaned, my head throbbing with the weight of my memories, recalling where I was. The stupid cave, with its jagged walls and ominous silence. I never should have come here. When was I going to learn that trusting my gut had only ever led to trouble? Regret gnawed at my insides as I struggled to make sense of my predicament, the damp air of the cave, suffocating.

I opened my blurry eyes, tried to sit up. Something yanked me back down hard, and I hit the wet, cold ground with a thud. After a failed attempt to use my arms, I realized I was tied up. Expertly by the feel of the bindings behind my back. I focused my running gaze on my legs, seeing the fishing net looped around my ankles for the first time.

Of course, it's a fishing net. How poetic.

"Finally," Stella said from the corner of the cave. "I thought you were a goner."

I sucked in a sharp breath between clenched teeth. "What happened?"

"What do you think?"

Muffled voices outside the cave carried in and I stopped breathing. My shoulders hiked up to my ears. I wiggled myself along a cave wall to right my body. It was the most uncomfortable position to be in, but at least I wasn't laid out on the ground anymore. Water trickled along the wall and fell into my collar, soaking my neck and back. *Wonderful.*

Shuffling steps echoed outside, and I jerked as they started toward me. My gaze zeroed in on the entrance to the cave and the sliver of light streaming in. A second later, two shadowy figures appeared before me, their faces obscured. I didn't have to see them to know they were Carla and Monica.

"She's awake," one of the women said. Carla, I assumed. She didn't seem to be the one in charge of the operation and the sheepishness in the voice gave her away.

The second woman growled something under her breath, then stepped closer, her features coming into focus. "I thought I told you to leave things alone?" Monica asked. When I didn't answer, she added, "You should have stayed out of this."

"The police think you're dead," I told Carla, ignoring the other woman. "I wanted to make sure that wasn't the case."

"That is kind of the entire point," Monica answered.

My eyes wandered from Monica to Carla. "It's why Monica tried to point me in her husband's direction, isn't it? You wanted the police to think he killed Robert and Carla." The women stayed silent. "It wouldn't have worked, you know. There'd be no evidence to tie your husband to the murder."

"We only need to buy time," Carla said.

"For what?" I asked. Then, recalling the rental agreement. "You were running away together. Disappearing. If the police spent their time chasing empty leads, you could get away. Avert their attention and make them think Carla was dead. No one would look for a dead woman in a rental property in the Grand Caymans."

Carla's face paled, and she side glanced Monica. "How did you know that?"

Next to her, the tall brunette scoffed. She walked over to the stack of books, giving the manila envelope a shove with her high heel. Her gaze seared into me. "Why would you leave it out in the open, Carla?"

"Really?" Robert's wife slapped her hands on her thighs. "I don't exactly have the luxury of a safe in here, do I? Besides, she never would have figured it out if you had stopped messing with her like I suggested."

"Messing with me?"

What in the latte gods was Carla on about? How did her girlfriend mess with me other than leading me astray when it came to Fallon? My thoughts swirled as I recounted the last few days on the island. Ah! The meeting that never happened when I nearly fell off the cliff chasing that ghost. Monica was supposed to meet us, then changed her mind. Back then, I thought it was because she was too afraid of her husband.

I shimmied to sit straighter. "In her defense," I told

Carla, "it pushed me to go after Fallon more. The break in, too. I take it one of you is responsible for trashing the villa to make it look like someone was looking for that safety deposit key. I'm sure the police are thinking the same I was, that Fallon is at fault. It was a good plan, except you didn't count on Collin finding out, did you? Is that why you killed him?"

"The creepy landlord?" Monica said with an eye roll. "No one is going to miss that imbecile."

"Monica, stop. Have some decency," Carla said. Her words shocked the other woman, her eyes bugging out of her skull like she had been slapped.

Trouble in paradise?

I decided to roll with it, keeping the women talking while I worked on loosening the net behind my back. The rough wall of the cave—while horrible for my back—was surprisingly useful. Every inch I moved sent a sharp slice across the ropes, slowly eating away at them. If I could distract the two long enough, I might have a shot.

In the least, I needed my hands free so I could attempt to use my magic to escape if things went south. Which I assumed they would, judging by past experience.

Another thought entered my mind. I stopped moving my wrists to look around the cave. *Where the heck is Stella Rutherford?* Hopefully, she left to warn

Joe and the police. How she planned on doing that was beyond me, but I had to give the ghost the benefit of the doubt and assume she didn't vanish for no reason.

Getting back to attempting to free myself, I trained a careful eye on the women. "Which one of you killed Collin then?" I spun to Monica. "I'm guessing it was you."

Surprisingly, it was Carla that answered. "Look, I know how this appears, but we truly didn't mean for it to go this far," she said. Her voice trembled, and she kept inching closer to Monica as she spoke. "There was no other way for us to be together. Not really."

"Divorce, maybe?"

Carla shook her head. "Not an option. Robert would have seen reason sooner or later, but not Fallon."

"You're telling me that your husband wouldn't let you divorce him?" I asked Monica. "I find that hard to believe."

"Well, believe it!" Monica hissed out. "You don't know Fallon. I wasn't his wife. I was his property. He would have ruined me if I embarrassed him. You read the prenup."

I shook my head, my chin dipping lower, rolling against the wall, my wrists slid apart further. A few more inches and I could slide them out of the net. I had to keep going. Staring Monica down, I said, "What you're saying is that you'd rather kill two innocent people than be broke."

Two vicious eyes burrowed into me as Monica seethed. She took one long stride away from Carla, then another. Continuing to watch me and making it impossible to keep working on the restraints, she bent down, her hand reaching for a pile of rocks nearby. Pushing one over, she dipped her arm inside and pulled out a shiny silver revolver.

The barrel pointed at my heart and my pulse raced in my veins.

"Monica, what the hell are you doing?" Carla yelped.

I gulped.

The gun barrel rose higher, aiming for my head.

The brunette's lips quivered, a smirk forming. "You said it yourself, babe. We don't have a choice."

"I-I don't think I can do this," Carla begged. "Let's just leave. By the time someone finds her, we'll be gone. Let's get out of here. Please."

Unwavering, Monica widened her stance, her finger on the trigger. "You don't really believe that, do you? She saw you, Carla. Any hope we had of the police thinking you're long gone is shot. Even if we do leave now, where will we go? She knows about the rental. We'd have go even further away. Are you ready for that?"

Come on, Carla. Use your heart. Or your head. Anything! I bit the inside of my cheek until I tasted blood. *Come on!*

Such wishful thinking. I watched as Carla's resolve withered before me and she took a few shaking steps toward her girlfriend, hiding behind her. The little coward.

"Sorry about all this," Monica said.

She didn't sound sorry at all.

I closed my eyes, tearing my wrists apart to free them. My magic rushed to the surface, but with my hands still trapped, there was no use. I couldn't aim anywhere and I'd only end up zapping myself in the butt if I used the electric current coursing through me now. My breath hitched. I ground my teeth together, waiting for the inevitable end.

"Duck!"

Stella's voice pierced the cave. I followed her command, dropping to my side and rolling on the ground. My eyes popped open, and I watched my familiar use every ounce of her power to throw a lettuce head at Monica's feet. The woman looked down, her eyes widening in confusion, finger still on the gun's trigger.

I stayed low to the ground, yelling out, "What are you doing?"

"We're not doing anything!" Carla shouted back.

I groaned. "Not you!"

The women exchanged twin looks of worry, Monica snapping out of it faster and pulling the gun on me again. She gave the lettuce head a little kick, and it rolled a foot away from her. Behind her, Stella floated with a grin on her face.

"I said duck!" she yelled again.

I had no clue what the ghost was going on about, but pushed my face into the ground for good measure. As I did, the scurry of tiny feet echoed through the cave. I peeled my face slightly off the ground to look up, shock thrumming through my system.

Running into the cave at a speed I couldn't predict were dozens of iguanas. I watched them trip over each other, their plump bellies bouncing as they fought to get to the large lettuce head Stella had tossed in here like a grenade. The ghost swerved left and right to avoid the stampede, grinning the entire time.

Unlike my familiar, Monica and Carla didn't anticipate the ambush. Their legs gave under them as the iguanas stomped through the cave. Monica lost her balance, toppling backward. Her finger jerked, and a gunshot rang out through the dim, cold space.

The bullet bounced off the wall over my head and

ricocheted back, passing directly through Stella's shoulder.

"Son of a!"

"Stella!"

The ghost held up two thumbs. "I'm fine."

I started to work on the fishing net again when another figure filled the lit entrance. Broad shoulders, messy devil-may-care hair, a stern expression. I'd know that look anywhere! My heart jumped for joy as Joe rushed into the cave. His eyes locked on me and he rolled his gaze over my body to make sure I was all right before running for Monica and Carla. Not breaking a sweat, because of vampire strength, he grabbed each one by the arm and yanked them back. The women shrieked, Monica dropping the gun in the process. Joe kicked it away with his foot, continuing to hold tight on the killers.

"Are you good?" he asked me.

I nodded.

He raised one questioning brow, and I shook my head to tell him I'll explain everything later. Righting myself, I leaned against the wall, saying, "Please tell me you brought the cops with you."

"Right behind me," Joe replied. Then, looking at the women he held in place. "You two are done."

I watched Carla break down into tears and Monica try to console her. A part of me felt bad for them. They must have been desperate to go to the extremes they went to simply to be together. I shook myself back to reality, reminding myself that all of this happened because Monica didn't want to lose the privileged life she had gotten used to. I wasn't sure what Carla's excuse was to go along with it, but love had a way of clouding one's mind.

Whatever the reasons were, it was over now.

An iguana smacked its tail into my leg and I laughed. What a vacation.

CHAPTER 25

Coconut and vanilla flavors swirled on my tongue as I gulped down the iced Coco-latte I'd made earlier. My legs stretched long on the beach towel, the sun warming them from above. Lounging under the shade of an umbrella, Joe flipped the pages of his book while he read. I lowered my sunglasses, looking at the water.

A crystal-clear blue as far as the eye could see. Simply perfect.

Swirling the straw in the glass, I took another sip, then set the latte down on the small table we'd dragged over from the backyard. Above our heads, planes zoomed every half hour, a fresh group of tourists coming to the island. I checked my watch as another plane flew by. Two more hours and we'd have to leave for the airport.

"Getting restless?" Joe asked.

I popped my sunglasses back in place, laying down again. "Not even a little. I'm going to miss this peace and quiet."

"We can always come back."

"Maybe we'll try a different place next time," I suggested. "One without so much drama."

Joe chuckled. "Less killing and more sunbathing. Got it."

He returned his attention to the book, his brow creasing in concentration. The water was still as a bath today, with only the slightest motion of the ocean as the waves came in to greet the sand. I rolled a smooth stone I'd found earlier between my fingers and settled onto my side to look across the beach. Despite the chaos of the last week, I meant what I said. I would miss the island.

After the police arrested Monica and Carla, things calmed down. Joe managed to change our itinerary again and extend the trip back to the original dates. We spent the last three days on the island doing exactly what we came here to do—absolutely nothing.

It was so relaxing that I barely even thought about what happened while we were here.

Of course, seeing Monica and Carla's face plastered all over the news every time we turned the television on didn't help. It appeared the women were up for lengthy trials and their lawyers were already gearing up for a sob story defense. "A fight for love," one headline said. I almost threw up when I read it and had to go into another room to meditate, so I didn't punch my fist through the screen. I was pretty sure that Collin's sister, who took over the rental properties, wouldn't appreciate me vandalizing the villa.

It seemed wherever we turned, exaggerated stories about the killing duo spread like wildfire. I supposed not much happened on this idyllic island and two murders back to back were the talk of the town.

I had to admit, it was quite the sensational story. Last we heard, Monica and Carla were being interviewed on all the major news stations from prison and there were even talks about a true crime documentary on one of the popular streaming networks.

Not to mention the spotlight the case put on Fallon Boatman. The developer was officially out of the real estate business and working on a book about the whole ordeal that was scheduled to come out in the new year. Playing the victim card worked in his favor. This morning, Joe saw that Fallon had already landed a four-book deal after this one. I had no idea what he would write about past the fiasco with his wife, or soon to be ex-wife, in jail, but there we were.

What worried me more was whether the women were going to get what they deserved. Island laws seemed to be very different from the ones we had in Orchard Hollow, so you really never knew.

I squinted at the sky. The sun hung lazily, casting a warm glow over the sandy shores of Oyster Bay. I let out a contented sigh. "Isn't this perfect? No mysterious deaths, no raccoons stealing treats, only the sound of the waves and the occasional squawk of a seagull."

Joe nodded in agreement. "It's been a long time since we both relaxed, I'd say."

Our moment of bliss was shattered when a shadow loomed over us, followed by a cacophony of squawks and flapping wings. Before we could react, a squadron of seagulls descended on us like a feathery tornado, their beady eyes fixed on their unsuspecting prey.

"Shoo!" Joe exclaimed, leaping to his feet and brandishing his book as a makeshift weapon.

I scrambled up to help, swatting at the dive-bombing birds. But the seagulls were relentless, swooping down to snatch the chips I'd brought out and sending snacks flying in all directions.

"Right when we thought we could enjoy a peaceful day at the beach," I grumbled as the last of the monsters flew off.

Joe surveyed the chaos with a mix of annoyance

and amusement. "Seems relaxation is not in our future after all."

With a contented sigh, I settled back onto the towel and Joe returned to his reading, the memory of the seagull attack already becoming a humorous anecdote in our wild vacation tale. A light breeze ruffled my loose curls, blowing them all over my face. I brushed the knotty mess away, clearing my sightline to find Stella hovering nearby. "Hi, Stella," I said with a smile.

"Try again," the ghost retorted, her hands on her hips.

I rolled my eyes and puffed my chest out with an annoyed sigh. "Hello, my brilliant familiar and savior of my life."

"Thank you for finally recognizing one of my many talents."

"Hello, Stella," Joe murmured.

The ghost drifted closer to my boyfriend, peering over the top of the book to see what he was reading. She nodded approvingly, a glimmer of mischief in her eyes. "I do love a well-read man."

I fought the smile spreading on my face, so I didn't give her the satisfaction of knowing she'd made me laugh. Stella needed a bigger head like I needed another ghost to follow me around. My eyes flicked to the edge of the water where the ghost that appeared this morning still lingered. Speaking of...

"What's her problem?" Stella asked, one thumb pointing at the woman in red.

The ghost floated with the tide, in and out of focus. Her long red gown, tattered and torn, touched the top of the water as she moved, feet dangling somewhere beneath all that fabric. The woman watched me closely, not saying a single word. Not that I could understand her if she did. So far, except for Stella and Isabella, I had no idea what the apparitions that came to me wanted.

I shrugged, leaning back on my forearms. "No clue," I told Stella. "She's been there since breakfast, though."

"Odd. Have you tried talking to her?"

"Absolutely not," I said. "It's our last day here, and I'd rather not waste it on a random ghost."

Joe sat up in his chair. "There's another ghost?"

"Nothing to worry about. Let's deal with my malfunctioning death magic later. For now, all I want is to—"

My fingers tingled and sparked in a blue glow. From them, an electric current stronger than I'd felt before, shot into the ground and I jumped, gasping. Joe was on his feet in seconds. I shook my magic-filled hands with little success of clearing away the energy.

Beyond me, close to where the woman in red floated, the air shimmered and tore.

"Run!" I shouted for her, but she didn't budge.

A rift the size of a truck split apart behind her. The woman's mouth opened wide a moment before she was dragged back, her red skirt trailing behind her. The rift shuddered like it took a deep breath. Suddenly, it was moving. Slowly creeping toward us and growing larger as it approached.

"Is that normal?" Joe asked.

My mouth gaped as I watched. It was definitely not normal. Eyes flaring, I jumped to my feet and got in front of Stella. My body in front of hers like a shield, I sucked in a breath as Joe came to stand beside me. "Get back, Stella," I warned my familiar. "Leave. Now."

There was no answer at my back.

I twisted to look over my shoulder, my heart hammering in my chest. Stella Rutherford was frozen. A single tear rolled down her cheek and her neck stretched, muscles taut. "I-I can't," she croaked out. "I can't move."

I turned to the rift and the darkness in it.

"Leave. Her. Alone," I growled out.

A deep laugh from the other side of the rift made the hair on my arms stand up. "Gladly, daughter of mine," Hades said.

Next to me, Joe snaked his fingers through mine.

"What do you want?"

"What every father wants," Hades replied. His voice was honey-dipped and smooth, a voice full of lies. "To see his only child."

I grimaced. "Well, I'm right here. You saw me. Good talk."

The rift widened, and I felt the familiar pull to go into it. I planted my feet wide apart, toes in the sand to keep me in place.

"The blood moon is nearly upon us," my father cooed.

"That's what this is about? The ritual isn't going to happen. Mom will stop it."

Another boisterous laugh. "No, my darling, she will not."

Want to bet? Hades clearly didn't know Sylvie Addison very well. When that woman had her heart set on something, there was no stopping her. I was about to tell him as much when he said, "You will host me on the blood moon, daughter of mine."

"Host you?" I cocked my head to the side. "You don't mean..."

"You will be my vessel," Hades confirmed. "Or your ghost will join the others."

The rift closed, the pull gone, and my father went with it. I leaned into Joe's side, checking for Stella behind us. Her eyes were wide and full of fear, but she was moving again. She was still free.

Gut twisting, I tucked a hair behind my ear and rubbed my forehead. Gran was right, life was an uphill battle and then you rolled. I looked at the ocean before me, the vastness of it, the infinity. What a way to end a vacation. We Addisons sure went out with a bang, didn't we?

COCO-LATTE

Ingredients:

· Unsweetened coconut milk
· Vanilla extract
· Salt
· Maple syrup
· Water
· Espresso

Instructions:

1. Combine 1 tbsp maple syrup with 2 shots espresso.
2. In a bowl, blend 1 can of coconut milk, a pinch of salt, and 2 tbsp of vanilla extract. Add water to thin out consistency (to taste) and use a handheld blender to froth the mixture.

3. Add ice to a tall glass.

4. Pour espresso mixture over the ice, follow with the coconut milk mixture.

5. Add whipped cream (to taste).

6. Swirl maple syrup to the top in a pattern of your choice.

7. Stir and Enjoy!

ABOUT THE AUTHOR

A.N. Sage is a bestselling, award-winning author of mystery and fantasy novels. She has spent most of her life waiting to meet a witch, vampire, or at least get haunted by a ghost. In between failed seances and many questionable outfit choices, she has developed a keen eye for the extra-ordinary.

A.N. spends her free time reading and binge-watching television shows in her pajamas. Currently, she resides in Toronto, Canada with her husband who is not a creature of the night and their daughter who just might be.

A.N. Sage is a Scorpio and a massive advocate of leggings for pants.

For more books and updates:
www.ansage.ca

Connect on social media:
Facebook Group:

facebook.com/groups/945090619339423/

Instagram:

instagram.com/a.n.sage/

TikTok:

tiktok.com/@ansagewrites

YouTube:

youtube.com/c/ANSageWrites